FOUR CORPSES IN A MILLION

This is the story of a master criminal
and his scheme to rule England. The
one thing he must have is money. Four
people have to die in order that his
plan might not be frustrated. This is
also the story of Roger Ferningham,
who cheated death three times — and
of Anne, who loved him. It is also the
story of Biggs, the Cockney, without
whom Roger could not have won
through . . .

JOHN ROBB

FOUR CORPSES IN A MILLION

Complete and Unabridged

LINFORD
Leicester

First published in Great Britain

First Linford Edition
published 2011

All characters in this Novel are entirely
imaginary and have no connection with
persons in real life.

British Library CIP Data

Robb, John.
 Four corpses in a million. - -
 (Linford mystery library)
 1. Criminals- -Fiction.
 2. Detective and mystery stories.
 3. Large type books.
 I. Title II. Series
 823.9′14–dc22

ISBN 978–1–4448–0637–3

Published by
F. A. Thorpe (Publishing)
Anstey, Leicestershire

Set by Words & Graphics Ltd.

1

The porter on duty at Blackwater Mansions was bored. There were two hours to go before the night porter came on. A long time to wait for his drink round the corner. It was cold outside this evening, cold enough to penetrate into the hall, where he waited beside the lift. Not that he minded the cold. He had had twenty years working a crane in a quarry on Dartmoor, so he knew what real cold was. When he had first taken this job he had been immensely pleased with it. There was a centrally heated flat in the basement, a lift which he could work sleeping, and a pub round the corner. No bachelor of forty-five could want much more, decided Biggs, even though he had to wear a uniform.

But of recent weeks he had felt increasingly bored, and tonight, despite the cold, he kept strolling out beyond the entrance doors in an unconscious effort to escape his surroundings.

As he emerged for perhaps the twentieth time, it was to find a stranger hesitating just outside.

Biggs looked at the stranger questioningly. Here, he thought, might be someone to talk to. He was right.

'It's some time since I was last in this district,' began the stranger, 'but there used to be a very good pub round here.' He peered up and down as he spoke, as though expecting a public-house to materialise suddenly in the middle of the mansions' flats.

'You probably mean the 'Craven Arms,' sir,' said Biggs. 'Not a bad place at all, not at all bad.' He was thinking as he spoke of two hours later.

''The Craven Arms,' eh? Yes, perhaps that's it.' The stranger seemed to be weighing something up in his mind, then: 'And whereabouts is this place? You wouldn't like to show me, would you? Perhaps you'd have time for a drink . . . '

Biggs glanced over his shoulder at the mansions. They did not look as though they would fall down for another ten minutes, he decided.

The trouble was that tenants were not allowed to work the lift. Ah, well, there were always the stairs, and ten minutes was not a long time.

'Don't mind if I do, sir,' he said to the stranger and fell into step beside him.

And so began a train of events which was to cost Biggs his job and a girl her life. For it was no accidental meeting, as Biggs imagined.

The saloon bar was cosy and the stranger very affable. At the third drink, Biggs thought he should be getting back. The stranger countered with another pint. Biggs accepted it.

The stranger then looked at his watch. 'Heavens, I've just got to put through a 'phone call,' he announced. 'I'll be back in three minutes.' He stopped at the counter long enough to get yet another pint for Biggs, and then left.

The porter sat on in a contented haze of warmth and beer.

In the meantime the girl had arrived at the mansions. She arrived at the vacant lift and read the notice: '*Tenants and visitors are requested not to use the lift unless accompanied by the porter.*' A second notice: '*To the Stairs* ☞' gave the uncomfortable alternative.

She rang the lift-bell and waited. Nobody came. With a shrug she turned to the stairs and mounted to the first floor. She turned to the left along the corridor, stopped at the first door, and knocked. It opened, and she stepped in.

Up to now the girl had shown no trace of indecision. That she was in a state of nervous excitement, the most casual of observers would have noticed. But now, as she first raised her eyes to the man who was closing the door upon her, her whole demeanour changed. She uttered a low gasp and shrank back until she reached the comforting support of the wall. Thereafter, with a face grown suddenly pale, she gazed at him with increasing panic.

But if the girl was horrified, the man at least was entirely composed.

'Good evening,' he said, bowing slightly. ''I must congratulate you on your — er

— self-control. It would have been a — nuisance if you had screamed, although, perhaps, almost natural — but now, of course, you are not going to do anything so — so stupid, shall we say?'

The girl continued to stare helplessly at him, as though she still could not believe her eyes.

A stranger happening in might indeed have wondered at the look of horror in her face. For the man at first glance seemed very ordinary.

Well below average height, thickset, bald, there was nothing at first to identify him from a thousand other middle-aged men. His mouth was full, his head round; and his eyes were so heavily lidded that he seemed on the point of falling asleep.

But it was as he spoke that one caught an atmosphere of dread. His eyes, though still half closed, seemed suddenly to menace. His full mouth, half opening, seemed to be moistly smiling, in evil contrast to the threatening eyes; whilst a cigarette, its end all chewed, hung from the lower lip.

He waited now a moment for the girl to

speak; then, as no sound came from her,

'You will sit down over there,' he went on, speaking very softly, 'and answer me a few questions.'

Another helpless look at him, and the girl moved over to a low chair by the table. Her step had grown suddenly tired, she seemed to move automatically. The little man took his stand by the window overlooking the street.

'Thank you. You came to see Major Ferningham by appointment tonight. You have his letter, of course?'

'His letter . . . '

'Yes! Yes! Please do not waste time. The — er — Major will be here in a few minutes, and I want to leave you here, ready to see him — or shall we say — for him to see you?'

The girl looked at him with a bewildered air for a moment, then opened her handbag, and taking out a letter, handed it over.

'Ah, yes — thank you. You will excuse me while I read it. Please do not move,' he added sharply as the girl made as if to rise.

'Yes, yes. I think the first page will be just sufficient. Put it back into your handbag, if you please. I will keep the rest, with your permission.' The girl rose from her chair, crossed over to his outstretched hand and taking the sheet of paper, put it back into her bag. Her movements seemed almost automatic.

'Thank you. I am so sorry you have had all this worry, but really, you should not meddle with other people's business. Let me see now. Ah, yes, the Major's revolver. I must not take that away with me, must I?' And as he spoke, the man withdrew a revolver from his overcoat pocket.

The girl shrank back at sight of it but he continued as though unaware of her.

'Noisy things, aren't they, unless of course you fit this on,' and his hand again emerged from his overcoat with a small metal object which he proceeded to screw on to the muzzle. So deliberate were his actions, that the girl seemed almost to be losing her fear, and leant slightly towards him, watching his movements.

'And now we will leave it, only first I must . . . ' Suddenly the girl saw! Her mouth opened, her eyes widening as they saw the revolver pointing, saw the finger move slightly! . . . There was a muffled report: she sagged suddenly, hideously, like a broken sawdust doll; then fell . . .

' . . . do that!' finished the little man as he looked down at her and at her fingers which stretched, closed, stretched, and then very slowly closed!

Unhurriedly, but with deft fingers, the man unscrewed the silencer, gave a slight rub with his gloved hand to the muzzle of the revolver where the marking showed, then dropped it on the further side of the body. Then with quick steps he crossed to the window, drew back the corner of the curtain, and looked down into the street. On the further pavement could be seen the vague outline of a man. As though in readiness for the movement of the curtain, the man in the street made a slight signal.

Behind the curtain the man in the room nodded with satisfaction, and moved back over to a writing desk in the far corner. Taking a small bundle of letters from the inside pocket of his overcoat, he tried the roll top. It was locked. In no way disconcerted, he drew a bunch of keys from his hip pocket, and set to work. At the fifth attempt the lock responded. He threw back the top, gave a casual glance inside, then tossed the bundle into a pigeon-hole and pulled the roll top back into position.

Again he crossed over to the window and looked out. A second signal passed; then crossing the room to the door, he opened it, and stood for a moment listening. The total absence of sound reassured him and he stepped out into the corridor, closing the door quietly behind him.

Without pausing, he made his way to the stairs, and descended them with a deliberate step. A minute later and he was in the street.

He turned to the right, walked along for a few yards and then crossed the road. The second man was now walking in the same direction. Except for them, the pavements were deserted. As the two drew level, the little man spoke without turning his head.

'The porter is quite safe?'

'Yes, sir. Still drinking, I think.'

'Good. It is not too dark to see from the telephone box?'

'No, sir. I tried it a few minutes ago.'

'Good. You had better get inside it. Our poor Major will be along any minute now. If anyone comes to the box, I shall walk past. You must start dialling but do not use any coppers. When you see me light a cigarette, ring the police. You know what to say?'

'Yes, sir, and I must really wait for them, sir?'

'Of course, of course! Do not be afraid. They will not recognise you — unless, of course, I had to remind them.'

There was a sudden silence; the other man seemed to shiver, then with an effort, he straightened himself.

'Very good, sir,' he said.

'Thank you,' the other answered softly. 'It is a great comfort that you are so reliable.'

Then with a suddenly altered manner:

'Go on, get into the box.'

The other quickened his step, reached

the telephone box a dozen yards away and stepped inside. The little man waited a moment, then turned half on his heel to face the road, and drew out a cigarette case. For a minute or so he waited, casually glancing up and down, then as a figure came into sight he stiffened slightly. For a full ten seconds he watched the stranger approaching on the opposite side, then he deliberately lit his cigarette. Inside the telephone box, the other man was already calling the police.

The Kensington Police Station was a bare hundred and fifty yards from Blackwater Mansions.

When the telephone bell rang, the sergeant on duty answered it with a bored air. As he listened, however, his attitude changed.

'What's that? Blackwater Mansions? Yes, yes, just round the corner. I know. Right! Hold on till we come.'

He turned from the receiver to the inspector by his side. 'Passer-by just rang up to say he heard a shot fired — in Blackwater Mansions, sir — a moment ago. First floor, he thinks.'

'Good Lord,' ejaculated the inspector. 'Here, Sergeant Williams. Take a couple of men immediately to first floor, Blackwater Mansions. Go carefully. Someone seems to be letting a gun off.'

'Right, sir.' The sergeant addressed was already leaving the room.

'Let me see,' went on the inspector, turning to the sergeant who had first taken the message, 'tell Doctor Harris and the ambulance to stand by in case they're needed. Be ready to 'phone St. Charles's Hospital, too. There may be a casualty. That's all.'

'Very good, sir!' the sergeant replied; then, as the door closed behind the inspector, 'That chap in the 'phone box seemed to think it was a case for the mortuary.'

Outside the station a car was already drawing up, although the distance was only a hundred and fifty yards.

The sergeant with two men tumbled in and barked out to the driver,

'You know the place? Right! Get along!' then settled himself forward.

In ten seconds they were outside the entrance.

'Should be a porter somewhere around,' muttered the sergeant. One of the men glanced in the office.

'Not here, sir,' he called out.

'Never mind. Peters! Stay down here. Don't let anyone by. Rogers, we'll take the stairs.'

They hurried up, two at a time.

'Thank the Lord he said first floor,' muttered Rogers, who was a heavy-weight. In spite of this he was on the landing first.

'Which door, sir?' he asked, pausing for his superior. By way of answer, the sergeant strode to the first door.

'Turnkey instead of Yale, luckily,' he muttered, inspecting the lock. Then taking hold of the door handle, 'Ready?' he asked over his shoulder. Rogers gave a nod. He was new to the Force, and could hardly speak for the sudden excitement which seemed to well in his throat.

The sergeant raised his right hand, beat sharply on the panel with his knuckles, and at the same time turned the handle of the door. It opened.

'Drop that,' he cried and sprang forward.

From behind, Rogers could only see a man in the act of turning to meet the sergeant. The next moment it was all over. Meeting with no resistance, the sergeant had steadied himself by clutching the right shoulder and arm of the man, and even as Rogers hurried forward, a revolver dropped to the carpet.

'Just a minute, just a . . . I was just going to ring you up!' exclaimed the man, though he made no effort to release himself.

'That's easy to believe,' the sergeant answered with an unusual sally of wit. He was agreeably surprised at the ease with which the situation had been met.

'Take charge of that revolver, Rogers,' he went on; then as the constable made to bend down: 'And use your handkerchief.'

The constable straightened himself, reddening at the words, then as he realised the use to which the handkerchief was to be put, his face cleared. 'Ah!' he grunted with understanding, fished a handkerchief out of his left trouser pocket, bent down again, and, with loving care, wrapped up the revolver, and straightened himself, his precious booty held proudly in both hands.

Up to this moment events had passed so swiftly that neither had done much more than glance round the room.

Certainly, as far as Rogers was concerned, his whole interest had been focussed on the stranger. That he was a gentleman was obvious. Not only his well-cut clothes, but his speech and his bearing left no trace of doubt. That he had offered no resistance was a little more surprising; that he retained his composure, although startled at first, was still more surprising. Rogers continued to stare in fascination at him, with a dim feeling that somewhere there had occurred an anticlimax, as if things had suddenly fizzled out.

The next moment he was recalled by the voice of the sergeant. 'Now take a look at the girl,' said the latter, releasing his grip on the stranger's shoulder, but still with a restraining hand on his right elbow. For the first time the constable looked past the men, past the table, and what he saw there fetched him up with a jerk . . .

On the further side lay the body of a girl. That she was dead, her unnatural posture left no room for doubt. He strode past the sergeant, and dropped on one knee beside her. She lay on her side, one arm beneath her, and the other stretched out stiffly at an angle. Her face was upturned, a look of horrified amazement frozen on it. Her mouth, probably attractive in life, was now drawn back in a surprised grin. A trickle of blood oozed from the corner. The constable felt suddenly sick. It was his first acquaintance with death by violence.

'Dead?' queried the sergeant.

'Yessir,' Rogers answered, and hardly recognised the voice for his own.

He forced himself to look again at the body, and as his gaze travelled down, he could see a pool of blood forming beneath her breast. He stretched out a shaking hand to turn her over, but the sergeant cut short his action.

'Better leave her alone then, until the doctor comes,' he said.

Thankfully the constable got to his feet. His legs were trembling slightly, and for the moment he had completely forgotten the precious revolver he carried.

'Look here, Sergeant,' broke in the stranger at that moment, 'this is all a ghastly mistake. My name's Ferningham, and . . . '

'Just a minute,' the sergeant interjected. 'Under the circumstances, I think it is my duty to warn you that anything you say may be taken in evidence against you.'

'Yes, that's all right, but I may just as well tell you now as later. My name's Ferningham. I'm the owner of this flat and this girl had an appointment to see me this evening. I had to . . . '

'One moment,' the sergeant inter-rupted, busying himself with pencil and notebook. 'You're . . . ' but the rest was left unsaid, for at that moment the door opened, to admit the inspector, followed by two other men. The sergeant straight-ened himself.

'Got here as ordered, sir. Left Peters downstairs; came in with Rogers. Found this man with revolver in hand, the girl lying dead over there, sir.

'Took possession of revolver (at this,

Rogers stepped slightly forward, vaguely holding out the handkerchief with its contents, but as no one took any notice, he hesitatingly retired again) and cautioned him,' went on the sergeant. 'He was just saying his name was Ferningham and that he's the owner of this flat, when you came in.'

The sergeant concluded his report and stepped back slightly, with a contented air.

'Right, Sergeant,' the inspector nodded appreciatively. 'Have you sent for doctor or ambulance?'

'No, sir,' he answered, subsiding a little. 'I was just . . . '

'Never mind, I brought Doctor Harris, in case . . . Will you have a look at her, Doctor? And Wilkins,' turning to the other man, 'tell them to bring the ambulance round. By the way, was the porter here when you came? He wasn't! Tell Peters as you go out to send the porter up directly he comes in, also to ask anyone going out to wait in the hall for me. Now, Mr. Ferningham, . . . ' turning to the owner of the flat. 'Major,' corrected the other with a faint smile.

'I am sorry — *Major* Ferningham.'

'That's all right. I quite understand, and I'd like to say something in spite of the sergeant's — er — caution. I'm the owner here, and I had an appointment with this — unfortunate — girl tonight. She used to be my secretary, and she wanted to see me about something . . . '

'Any idea what it was about?' the inspector broke in.

'I'm afraid not,' the other resumed. 'I just came in a few moments ago, and found her exactly as she is now. I saw a revolver on the floor, picked it up, and just at that moment your sergeant came in.'

'Why did you pick up the revolver?'

'Well, it — er — looked like my own and I was just examining it to see if it was.'

'And it was?'

'Yes. I keep it in the drawer of this table,' pointing to a small rectangular table in the corner.

'H'm.' The inspector's face showed no trace of his thoughts.

'Were you alone when you came in? Did anyone see you?'

'Yes and no,' Ferningham answered carefully. 'The porter was not there when I came in.'

'I see. Well, I'm afraid that under the circumstances you will have to go along to the station, sir. Sergeant, will you accompany Major Ferningham to the station? I'll be along there later.'

'Very good, sir,' and the sergeant motioned Ferningham to the door. In silence they took the lift, but Ferningham was thinking furiously. At the moment he certainly *looked* to be in as awkward a mess as he could possibly hope for. He was under no illusions as to the inspector's opinion, polite though his words had been. The two police standing in the hall seemed to emphasise his position. They had been talking to a rather short man in a dark overcoat, but at sight of the sergeant they came forward.

'This is the man who first gave the alarm from the 'phone box, sir,' the foremost explained.

'Ah,' said the sergeant, 'you had better take him up to see the inspector.'

Ferningham cast an interested glance at the man. He had been wondering how it was that the police had happened to arrive at that moment. Apparently this man had given an alarm of some sort. Seemed nervous enough, anyway. Probably imagined he was near a desperate criminal, he thought bitterly.

The journey to the station was uneventful, and after about an hour's delay Ferningham was allowed to make a statement. He was then formally charged with the murder of the girl Rosemary Webb, by shooting her with a revolver, and that night he slept in a prison cell.

2

'Gentlemen of the Jury, are you agreed upon your verdict?'

'We are.'

'Do you find the prisoner guilty, or not guilty?'

'Guilty, my Lord.'

The judge settled himself forward slightly, and rearranged a fold of his robes. He was very old; so old, that his hands and his deeply lined face seemed unnatural, seemed dead. Only his eyes were alive in that heavily lined mask.

When at last he spoke, it was with careful enunciation, each word pronounced separately and distinctly as water drips on stone. He seemed to be husbanding his strength.

'Roger Ferningham, you have heard the verdict of the Court. Have you anything to say as to why I should not now pronounce sentence upon you?'

The prisoner in the dock moved

slightly forward and rested his hands on the ledge before him. He was entirely composed; and only his whitening knuckles showed anything of the strain which he must be undergoing. He glanced down at his counsel with a tired smile.

'My Lord, no one, I am quite sure, regrets this tragic mistake more than I. In a few moments it will be your painful duty to sentence me to death for a crime of which I am innocent. And so another murder will be committed.

'My Lord, I am convicted of the murder of my former secretary. She was killed in my flat, with my revolver.

'She had written letters, desperate letters, to someone. No name is mentioned. These letters are found in my flat, unfortunately for me, therefore they are my own. In her handbag was found part of a letter written by me to her, urging her not to take desperate steps; the rest of the letter is not there, again unfortunately for myself.

'A witness has testified that he heard a shot. The police arrived and I was found some minutes after, standing over her body, the revolver in my hand. 'The evidence,' to quote the counsel for the prosecution, 'is overwhelming.' He should have said 'too overwhelming.'

'The prosecuting counsel was pleased to call me a man of brains. If this be true, then this evidence is not.

'Those desperate letters, written to an unnamed person, kept in a bundle just inside the desk, is that the action of a man of brains?

'To shoot a girl in one's own flat and then to stand for several minutes over her body, revolver in hand. Would a man of brains conceive such gross stupidity?

'Of motive, my Lord, you have none. The prosecuting counsel has called it a crime of passion. My Lord, I do not inspire passion in my secretaries. But there, I will not waste your time with arguments which to me appear so obvious but which other gentlemen,' with a quiet glance at the jury, 'have not been able to grasp. And if I appear a little prejudiced in my own favour, you must remember that I have knowledge instead of evidence.'

He paused for a moment, and once again glanced at the jury with his quiet smile.

By now there was dead silence in the Court. The jury were in the throes of discomfort. The nearest man in the front row had turned away from that smile, biting his under lip until the blood came. A second man, handkerchief in hand, had paused half-way in the act of wiping the perspiration from his brow, seemingly unable to move, so that little drops were already beginning to run down into his thick eyebrows. The solitary woman seemed about to faint. Only the foreman gazed back steadily at the prisoner.

For an instant their eyes held each other, then the prisoner, summoning up his strength to maintain his self-control, continued.

'And so, my Lord, you will presently do your duty. But meanwhile, I warn you that this girl was murdered by someone, and that someone was not I. That those letters found in my desk were not mine, but deliberately placed there by someone who, for some terrible reason, intended that I should die.

'Therefore, in sentencing me, you are allowing a murderer to escape, and out of this, my Lord, other murders will follow.'

He finished. Of what happened thereafter he had no clear knowledge. Dimly through a haze, he saw the Court room, heard the judge's voice ' . . . and careful trial . . . taken from there to a place of . . . hanged by the neck . . . soul.'

And then he was led below.

3

The trial was three weeks old, and once again the newsboys were busy.

'Late extra speshul! Ferningham appeal. Result!'

Twopence a quire profit — twopence for every twenty-four people who stopped to read how Ferningham had had his sentence commuted to penal servitude for life!

Lucky devil, some people said, while others, who knew a little about the law, wondered why the man had not pleaded a sudden quarrel in the first place to try for a verdict of manslaughter.

And while that evening the newsboys were calling the result, a train was steaming out of Paddington Station. Although it was an express, the centre coach was not a corridor one. One compartment in particular had drawn blinds and was locked. Inside were three men, two of whom were uniformed, and in the services of H.M. Prisons. Between them sat the third, Roger Ferningham, for the last time for a very long while was wearing a lounge suit.

'Nasty night, Bill,' said the man on the left, and lifted his hand to the cigarette in his mouth. There was a slight clink as he did so, and Ferningham's left arm moved.

'Sorry,' said the warder, letting his arm fall. 'I ought to be used to it by now. It's against the rules, but would you like a cigarette?'

'Thanks,' Ferningham answered gratefully. 'This is really far less embarrassing than I thought it would be.'

Thereafter he said no more for a long time, while the train continued to roar through the gathering night.

The man on the right who had been addressed as Bill was the next to break the silence.

'Penny for your thoughts,' he asked the prisoner sympathetically.

'I'm afraid,' the latter replied, 'you must have grown tired by now of listening to explanations of innocence.'

'Well,' said Bill thoughtfully, 'there are

some that take it hard, and some that take it harder. But it all comes to the same in the end, and the less you think about it the better it'll be, I reckon. Isn't that so, Charlie?' turning to the other warder.

The other nodded without speaking, and silence again descended. But the conversation, brief as it had been, had had the desired effect. Ferningham forced himself to cease brooding over his position, and endeavoured to take some interest in the faint glimpses he could catch of the stations they were passing through.

'That's Slough, isn't it?' he exclaimed as the express hurtled through a station. 'Changed a bit since I was here last.'

'Ah,' said Charlie, stung to volubility at what was obviously an old grievance. 'And not for the better, neither. Thousands of them houses rushed up, planted anywhere; what'll they be like in a few years' time is what I'd like to know! Jerry-built, that's what they are. I was in the trade meself before the war, and it comes crool 'ard to see what they're putting up now.'

29

'Same all over the country, Charlie,' Bill broke in. 'Can't pick on Slough particularly. Why, I've got a cousin down Ealing way, decent chap he is, though you wouldn't think it to listen to his wife.

'He saved up some money about three years ago and put twenty-five pounds down on one of these what you call semi-detached villas. Last year he had to spend thirty pounds on the roof, then this year there comes a crack in the bathroom wall. Funny thing was that the bathrooms of both houses were next to each other, and when the crack came, up by the top, you could see through easily if you got your eye up against the wall. Jack's missus didn't notice the crack, being the sort of woman that always walks about with her eyes on the floor, looking to pick up something; but she did notice that Jack was having baths three times a week, which was more than he need to, being so that he's in the Town Hall, and not a job where he gets dirty. Anyway, the next thing she notices were his footmarks on the edge of the bath, and then it was all up.

'Only made matters worse, too, when Jack said that the only washing he'd seen next door was clothes being washed in their bath because she said that wasn't his fault, anyway, and where there was a will there was a way, and if he'd had any respect for her at all, instead of trying to shame her, he'd've denied it, even though he knew she knew all about it.'

'Not too good for Jack,' said Ferningham politely.

'Oh, he knows how to handle her, does Jack. He soon headed her off by wondering who would have to mend the wall — him or the people next door. That started her off, and as far as I know they're still arguing with the other. Jack's missus says that it belongs to the others becos they bought their house first, so Jack and she only bought what was tacked on to them.'

'Ah,' said Charlie, with all the insulted pride of one who had been in the trade, 'she pitched on the right word there. 'Tacked on,' and no mistake! Green wood warps in three months; mortar and concrete what crumples becos they've been too stingy with the cement! Push 'em up, that's all they think, and the Government talks about slum clearance, and watches them there Council Estates being run up. Don't ask me!' And as neither of the other two seemed inclined to ask him, he relapsed into silence once more.

By now the train had roared through Maidenhead, and was even about to enter the Twyford cutting . . .

Ten minutes before, a goods train had left Reading and was even now passing through Twyford . . .

On the footboard of the express the stoker had laid aside his shovel for a moment and was bending down to pick up a thermos flask behind him. He straightened himself, unscrewed the metal cup, filled it with tea, and, turning, held it out to the driver. 'Cup of tea, Joe?' he asked, when the driver suddenly leant out of the cab. Wondering, the stoker leant out too.

'Oh, God, NO!!' he cried futilely, and the next moment there was a crash! . . .

On the bridge which spans Twyford

cutting, just above the town, two people were leaning against the parapet, idly looking down on the rails. They were about to turn away, when they heard the blast of the express's whistle. 'Let's see the express go through,' said one. Instead they saw a sight they would never forget.

As the engine of the express came into sight, a goods train thundered beneath them, and the next moment they met head to head with a terrifying crash!

Both engines reared up at the impact, grotesquely unreal in the night shadow, then as the full effect of the express's speed became felt, the goods engine fell sideways, whilst that of the express dropping down on to its front wheels again, for all the world like a rearing horse regaining its footing, continued on its way, ploughing a path through the tangled heap which a moment before had been trucks. Behind it the coaches, telescoping one into the other, were literally falling into pieces . . .

The sound was unearthly, titanic! The first crash seemed not so much to be followed, as to lengthen itself into an ever-increasing medley of clamour. The bridge itself rocked with the vibration. And then, even as the two watchers stood, rooted to the spot, deafened by the din, flames began to shoot up . . .

Half a mile away in the signal box the signalman was bending over his levers weeping like a child!

Back in the compartment, Charlie had just recommenced his tirade against modern architecture.

'And if all what is said is true,' he argued fiercely, 'they don't even use a plumb-line on the walls half the time. Just lean over the side and 'spits' I'm a-told; and . . . '

At that precise moment came a sound louder than Ferningham had ever heard in his life. Simultaneously the floor gave a heave, and the compartment seemed to fold up! For one second Ferningham felt himself falling forwards, then sideways and backwards until he seemed to be standing on his head; then, to his distorted view, the whole compartment seemed to fall to pieces; there came a sudden blackness, and he knew no more . . .

Already up and down the line black forms were emerging, some staggering to the side, there to collapse upon the grass verge, others running aimlessly to and fro, others just standing there. Already the bridge over the cutting was crowded, and people could be seen hurrying up and down the banking. From the tangled heap of débris arose a medley of cries, shrieks and groans, the hiss of escaping steam, and minor crashes and thuds as the wreckage settled down. All this, together with rapidly spreading flames which had started from the coalbox of the express, combined to make the scene a veritable inferno!

Darkness, complete and utter darkness, was Charlie's first impression after that first terrifying crash! The next moment he realised that something soft was completely enveloping his head; he started to move, but there was a dreadful weight across his shoulders. Simultaneously came a searing pain which stabbed his left side. He lay still for a moment whilst his brain cleared slightly. He seemed to be lying face downwards and spread-eagled, with something which pinned him across the shoulders. He tried to move again and found the weight shift slightly. At the same moment consciousness returned with a rush! There had been a train wreck, he was imprisoned beneath the wreckage! Dimly he could hear cries and shouts, and as if pricked into action he made another effort to wriggle free . . . Again that searing pain! The sweat broke out on his forehead . . . Cunningly he twisted slightly sideways to ease that sharp stab, and recommenced his efforts. He was able to move slightly, and the next instant his head was clear of the enveloping folds.

But still he could not move his right arm, it was chained by his wrist beneath the wreckage.

Chained! As the word passed through his brain, memory came back with a rush. He was handcuffed to Ferningham, who lay somewhere beneath the wreckage.

At the same moment his mouth and nostrils, no longer enveloped by cloth, breathed in smoke! Blind, unreasoning panic seized him! The wreckage was on fire.

'Oh, God, don't let me burn,' he sobbed hysterically, and scrabbled in the dirt with his free hand.

For nearly half a minute he lay there, moaning and crying, unable to think. Then gradually he regained his self-control. The key was in his left-hand trouser pocket. Slowly, for every movement caused fresh pain in his side, he worked his way into his pocket and with trembling fingers withdrew the key. Slowly again, and still more slowly, he twisted and strained until his side was red-hot with agony, whilst he worked his left hand along his right arm.

'Don't let me drop it, don't let me drop it,' he sobbed. His left hand was out of sight now beneath the wreckage, past his right cuff. He felt the chill of steel, could hear amongst all that medley of sound the faint scratching of the key on the metal, then click, something gave, and the next moment the weight of the handcuff fell loosely across his wrist! He was free . . .

For a moment he lay there shivering and retching violently, unable to lift his head from the ground. Then, as his senses cleared, he gathered himself for a last effort and, wriggling sideways and backwards, he got clear of the débris. He rose to his feet, swaying dizzily, tottered for half a dozen yards, then, as he remembered his companions, he turned as if to go back. The effort was too much and he collapsed in a dead faint.

By now order was beginning to emerge from chaos. Already the banks of the cutting were being lined with the forms of injured people. Here and there piles of luggage were already beginning to collect under the watchful eyes of their owners.

Along the line of wreckage several small bands of rescuers had formed and were searching to release those still imprisoned in the tangled mess of débris.

One such band had just arrived opposite the point whence Charlie had emerged.

The leader stooped for a moment, his hand on the end of the very beam which had pinned Charlie, and looked underneath the heaped-up wreckage.

'Something under there!' he exclaimed. His voice was muffled by the handkerchief round the lower part of his face as protection against the ever-increasing volume of smoke. At his words and signals three others sprang forward to the beam and pushed upwards at it, using it as a lever to raise the rest. It rose about a foot. The leader signalled to the fifth member to tie a handkerchief round his face and take his place at the beam.

'Try to raise her a bit more, boys. I'm going to get under it,' he said, and forthwith, getting on to his knees, he started to crawl beneath the pile. Choking and gasping, the others heaved against the beam. The flames were already on the further side of the wreckage, and the heat was intense.

Only the leader's legs could be seen now.

'Heavens, he must be getting right into the flames,' exclaimed one of the others, and then —

'Hurry up, man,' he called thickly to the leader.

One of the men at the beam released his left hand for a moment to rub his smarting eyes and the beam dropped an inch.

'Hold it, blast you!' came from behind him.

'Tell him to come out,' grunted a third. 'He'll be done for in another moment.'

Then a muffled voice could be heard from the leader. 'Catch hold of my legs and pull!'

'Catch hold of his legs there, someone,' went up a chorus.

A man from behind hurried forward to their help and crawled underneath, too.

The remainder gave a last heave to the beam, raising the mass another four inches.

'Hold it, they're coming,' was the cry. A fresh volume of smoke eddied round them. They could only see about a foot away.

'Tell them to hurry,' called out the third man again. 'I can't hold . . . much more!' His voice was rising with a note of panic.

But it was nearly over, and the next moment the shoulders of the leader and the men who had gone to his aid came into view. Half a minute later and they emerged, dragging a third between them.

'Right,' called out the foremost on the

beam. 'Let her down!' The other obeyed thankfully and turned away coughing and gasping to help with the rescued victim.

His arms were limp, his coat was in shreds, the shoulders blackened by smoke and fire. As two men lifted him they turned him over so that his face was revealed for the first time.

'Good God!' exclaimed one of the bearers, and nearly dropped him in horror.

'Here, hold up!' the other said fiercely, 'and don't be a darned fool!'

Shivering, the other obeyed, his face averted from the sight. Stumbling, they carried him to the grass verge and laid him down. The bearer, who had adjured the other not to be a fool, knelt down beside him.

'Pretty far gone,' he announced, 'but he's alive. Don't know exactly how far gone, though.' The face was a terrible sight. There were two long gashes, which had bled freely until the smoke or flames — it was difficult to tell which — had blackened both the face and the congealing blood. The hair was singed to powder, which came away at the touch of a handkerchief.

'Better get him in one of the first ambulances,' concluded the bearer as he got to his feet. 'Be touch and go in any case, I should think!'

And so a quarter of an hour later Roger Ferningham, badly burned and unconscious, was put in an ambulance en route for the Berks and Bucks County Hospital, an unknown victim.

4

Pain! Wave upon wave of searing white-hot pain!! Seconds like hours, lengthening into days, while nerves seemed to live only to torture the more; cold sweats of exhaustion, with merciful hours of total unconsciousness.

There was no time, only oblivion in a cycle of pain!

★　★　★

'Better see the new grafting case first, Sister. No. 14, isn't it? Temperature chart? Ah, thanks . . . h'm . . . collapsed. Eh? When's his next saline due? Twelve o'clock? Bottles, blankets? Yes . . . nothing much more you can do. Hasn't been conscious at all, has he? No, well — six o'clock should show one way or the other.'

★　★　★

'No. 14, Sister? . . . Ah, yes; temperature chart? . . . Thank you! 97.4. Ah, that's better! Going up nicely. I think we can take him off salines now! How's the pulse? . . . Oh, much stronger! Oh, yes, he's going on very nicely . . . '

'Wonder who he was. Let me see, we'll have those bandages off in another five days. Be able to see what he looks like then . . . Expect he'll get a shock, he'll probably look quite different . . . Ah, well, let's hope we'll have made him better looking! . . . Now what about No. 15? . . . '

There was a dull, confused murmur, and a red haze! His face felt one mass of soreness! He was by the sea, and the sun had caught it! He could hear the sea more plainly now! He wanted to move, to hide his face from the sun, but he was too tired! . . .

★ ★ ★

He was cold and stiff! He mustn't sleep any more, he must get up. But something held him and his face was so sore. Ferningham opened his eyes, but there was no sea. Why did he think he was near the sea, anyway?

He was in a room, in bed. What room? What bed?

He lay still for a minute, trying to think. His face ached badly, and there seemed to be a tightness across his chest.

What had he been doing? He had gone to work that morning, and then . . . and then . . . something dreadful . . . he couldn't think! . . . Sentence of the Court be . . . Yes, yes, he had killed someone! Yes, no . . . no, he hadn't, but they had made him guilty . . . Well, where was he? . . . He was in a train and then . . . He couldn't think any more! But he must . . . There had been a lot of noise, yes, there must have been an accident . . . That was it, a train smash! . . . Then where was he now? . . . In hospital? . . . He looked cautiously to his side, he could not see further, and his head seemed fixed. There should be a policeman by his side! . . .

They always did that when there had been an accident to a prisoner! . . . No, he wasn't there.

45

Perhaps he had gone out for a minute!
. . . Yes, he had gone to have a cigarette
. . . Of course, that was it, you couldn't
smoke in a hospital ward . . . Pity, he
would have liked to . . . They had given
him one in the train . . . Decent chaps,
both of them . . .

He pursed his lips slightly as though he
were smoking a cigarette. The movement
brought pain to his face . . . He must
have been badly hurt . . . Where was
everyone? Why didn't they come and tell
him how badly he was hurt?

Ah, there was someone now! . . .

'No. 14, Sister? . . . How's he this
morning? . . . Hallo! . . . He's coming
round! . . . Ah, that's better. How do you
feel? . . . Never mind, don't talk now! Just
keep quiet. You've had an accident . . .
Going to be all right! Yes . . . Just keep
still! Yes, it's bandaged! . . . Better have a
nurse here for a time, Sister. Yes, keep an
eye on him. He may try to move those
face dressings.'

★   ★   ★

46

'Going to be all right.' Ferningham had wanted to ask them a lot of things, but he was too weak . . . It would do later, anyway.

When Ferningham next woke it was afternoon, though he did not realise this at first. He felt definitely stronger, however, his extreme exhaustion had passed. With it, however, came increasing realisation of his position, and as he lay there, vaguely aware of the nurse who sat beside him, his chief feeling was of despair. To have gone through, to be still going through such pain and discomfort in order to be saved to work out his sentence, it was an ironic position.

There was a movement beside him, as the nurse noticed his return to consciousness.

'Had a nice sleep, No. 14? How do you feel now? You've been very lucky, you know, and now you've got to lie quiet and get strong.'

'I don't feel too bad,' answered Ferningham slowly, 'except for my face, Nurse. What's the matter?'

'You were burnt a little and you're all

bandaged up, that's all. You mustn't mind it being sore for a time, and don't touch your bandages, will you? Now I'll just fetch Sister. You'll have to tell us who you are, you know, so that we can let your friends or relatives know about you . . . '

'Friends, relatives! . . . ' queried Ferning-ham, quite bewildered.

'Why, yes! You've been here four days, and they'll be very worried. We couldn't find out anything about you, you see. Your face was . . . was cut about a little, and we can't publish a photograph of a head in bandages, can we?' The nurse giggled slightly, and then, realising that she was behaving very unprofessionally, reverted immediately to type and sailed away to fetch the sister.

Ferningham lay there, his mind still in a daze.

He was unknown! By what freak of chance it had all happened, he did not know; but for the present it was enough. He was not an injured prisoner, he was a patient whose friends and relatives must be worrying about him! For a moment he felt free, and, so doing, felt well enough to get up and go; the next — he was back in the throes of despair. It could not last! As soon as his face was well enough, he would be recognised! He could not even understand how he had escaped recognition when first rescued. Unless his face had been so badly hurt! ... In which case, supposing he was scarred, scarred in such a way that his face was completely changed; disfigurement would be but a small price to pay for freedom. He lay there, thoughts racing through his brain, until the perspiration stood out on his forehead. The mental effort was proving too much for his weakened condition.

But even while he wearily decided to let things take their course, thoughts were humming in his head. The sister would be there in a moment. What was he to tell her? That he knew no one, had no relations, that was essential. That he was out of work? Yes, or else they would want to let his employers know! He felt faintness coming over him, and fought it back desperately. The sooner he had told his tale, the better. Thank heavens, the sister was coming at last.

She paused beside him, and with a critical eye, perceived immediately that he was excited.

'You mustn't excite yourself, No. 14,' she said, not unkindly. 'You've been quite lucky, you know, and you're going on very nicely.'

Ferningham nodded slightly.

'I'm all right, Sister,' he said in a voice which belied his statement.

'Yes, yes, but you've got to be quiet. Now could you just tell me anyone you want us to get in touch with, and then I won't bother you any more.'

'Thank you, Sister, but I don't think there is anyone . . . I haven't any relatives, at least none that I know of, and no friends particularly . . . I was going down to Oxford to see if I could get a job; I haven't one at the moment . . . but that will have to wait for a week or two.'

'I see!' The sister was obviously discontented to meet someone who had neither friends, relatives, nor employment.

'Well, if you can just give me your name for our records, then we needn't bother you any more, because you must rest, you know.'

'David Garrett, sister, if that helps, though as for address, I've got nothing permanent.'

'David Garrett? Thank you,' and as the nurse returned with the sedative, 'and now you just drink that, and then be quiet!'

Ferningham obeyed. He could hardly realise that it was over for the moment.

Dazed, he watched the retreating figure of the sister, then with a lighter heart than for a long time, he relaxed and gave himself up to sleep.

★　★　★

The next few days passed swiftly. For half the time Ferningham slept, so much were his exhausted nerves in need of rest, and though he still suffered considerably from the facial injuries, yet his naturally strong constitution enabled him to overcome the pain with fair success.

On the eighth morning of the accident, he was told that the dressings were to be taken off. For a moment he failed to realise the importance of this, and was mildly surprised at the sister's unwonted nervousness. Chaffing her slightly, he asked the cause. She was silent for a moment, then:

'Well, No. 14, now you're so much better, I'm going to tell you that you were in quite a bad way when you came here. The subcutaneous tissues of your face were burned, and the surgeon had to do a grafting operation, so you mustn't be surprised if you don't recognise yourself at first. Anyway, a nice new face will be quite a change, and though you'll look like a boiled lobster at first, that won't be for long.' To her great relief the patient showed no signs of dismay. In fact, he even showed signs of relief, as he answered: 'If that's all that's worrying you, Sister, you can start as soon as you like. You have the first look, then warn me what to expect before you hand me over a looking-glass.'

'Anyway, if it's a very great improvement, we shall make a special charge,' she smilingly replied, and moved on to await the doctor.

In a quarter of an hour the latter arrived, and the process of removing the dressings was begun. Though necessarily tedious, there was surprisingly little discomfort for Ferningham. With a final 'Now don't move those facial muscles at all, just let them relax!' the surgeon straightened to examine his handiwork. He was obviously gratified.

'Quite satisfactory, I think,' he said, turning to the doctor beside him.

'Very healthy graft, sir,' the other replied, leaning forward. 'Congratulations.'

'Well,' said Ferningham, 'what do I look like, gentlemen?'

'Chiefly like a peony at the moment,' the surgeon answered jovially, 'and I'm afraid you'll have to be as dumb as one for the next few days,' he went on, turning to his colleague. 'Ointment dressings for seven days, I think — better use gauze — and then I'll have another look at it. I don't think it will die. If it does, let me know at once.' He became aware of the agitated signals from the patient, who was obediently refraining from speech.

'Oh, I see, no, no, I didn't mean *you*

might die,' he said quite cheerfully. 'It was referring to the graft. Now and again, you know, skin doesn't take kindly to being moved, and decides to stop functioning. In which case, of course, we put another patch on the function.' The little gathering of doctor, sister and nurse round the bed chuckled obediently at the jest, as a well-trained court laughs dutifully at its judge's quips. Having received his due meed of applause, the surgeon concluded, 'but yours looks as if it will stand the strain all right. Good morning.'

5

A rattle of cutlery showed that it was 12.15 p.m. in the hospital. Ferningham, sitting up in bed arrayed in a grey flannel bed-jacket of uncertain age, glanced at the nurse who was dropping a knife, a spoon and two forks on the locker by his side.

'Don't tell me there's a pleasant change today — rice pudding, perhaps?'

'Rice pudding, *and* a pleasant change,' she answered with a grin. 'Some sultanas have got mixed up in it.'

'H'm! At school we used to call it the 'Yellow Peril.' It'll be a sad day for schools and hospitals if India and China stop cultivating rice.'

'I expect we shall grow our own then,' she answered gaily.

'Heh! No. 7, you get back into bed immediately. *You* know what . . . Good gracious, is your bed on fire?' She hurried across the ward and pulled back the sheets and blankets. A cloud of tobacco smoke was released. She stood for a moment biting her lips, in a vain endeavour not to smile. 'Now I wonder how it came there now?' said the latter occupant in a small voice. ''Tis someone under the bed, I'm thinkin'.'

'It's where you'll be, No. 7, if you don't get back immediately; and no more smoking or I shall report you.'

The ward rocked with applause as the nurse made her exit.

Ferningham, left to himself, stroked his face gently. The oil dressings had been off now for three days, and his face, except that it had two or three faintly red patches, was apparently normal. As an operation, in fact, the grafting and building up had been an incredible success, although Ferningham had received the shock of his life when he had first been allowed a mirror. Whereas he had been frankly plump and full faced, he was now decidedly lean, with prominent cheek bones and a much longer upper lip. His eyebrows, once high and arched, now seemed almost to veil his eyes. His nose seemed slightly longer and very slightly Roman. Small differences taken separately, but together they caused such an alteration that for the moment he had been unable to realise it was his own reflection in the glass.

His eyes lit up as his meal was placed before him; it was chicken, and plenty of it, a very pleasant change. The rice which followed, however, was allowed to grow cold by his side. He sighed wistfully as he thought of the food he had been accustomed to eat in the past; he had not imagined so much rice existed. Then, as he thought of the next few days, his heart sank a little. He was literally quite penniless. As to whether his goods and chattels were forfeit to the Crown, he was uncertain; vaguely he seemed to remember that the Crown took over murderers' estates, but he could not be quite sure. In any case, however, he could not touch a thing. To the world in general he was dead in the railway accident, and unless he wished to finish his twenty years in gaol, he would have to steer very clear of his place.

For the moment he had presumably one set of underclothes and one suit, probably very damaged. He turned to the nurse who had arrived to clear away the plates and said:

'Are my clothes up yet, Nurse? I'm getting up this afternoon, aren't I?'

'You'll get them in about half an hour,' she promised him, 'though heaven knows they'll be too big for you if you leave your food like this.'

When eventually they arrived, however, the coat and shirt were missing as they had been too badly damaged to be retained. A coat and shirt were loaned him in their place, the one too big and the other too small, but Ferningham was in no mood to quibble. As soon as he had dressed himself and walked a trifle unsteadily to the day ward, he had felt an urge to be out of the place. It seemed incredible that he really could walk out free and unmolested; and although he kept reassuring himself, yet something akin to panic bade him get out while the going was good. With this end in view he waylaid the sister.

'Oh, Sister,' he said with genuine eagerness, 'I feel very fit, you know. How soon do you think I can get my discharge?'

'Oh, very soon, I should think,' she answered non-committally. 'Perhaps next week, or the week after!'

'Next week!' he exclaimed in dismay. 'I was thinking I could be getting along tomorrow.'

'Well, there's no harm in thinking, No. 14,' she replied, 'but I don't think we shall be losing you just yet.'

'Well, couldn't I see the doctor tomorrow?' Ferningham asked in desperation.

'You can always see the house surgeon,' the sister proffered formally. 'If you care to see him tomorrow morning, he'll be able to tell you more than I can.'

'Thanks very much then, Sister, if you'll fix that for me,' said Ferningham warmly, ignoring her formal manner.

But the interview the following day proved more difficult than he had expected.

'My dear chap,' the house surgeon

expostulated, 'you may not realise it, but from a medical point of view you're a case in a lifetime. Apart from the fact that you were a thousand to one against surviving the shock, the grafting is, speaking as one who did not do it, a perfect example. So although I needn't tell you that we haven't the slightest fear of any complication arising from the graft, yet, in such exceptional cases, we like to watch it out to the bitter end.'

Ferningham renewed his appeals, whereupon the house surgeon went on:

'Of course, if you really insist, then we can't keep you here. You'll have to sign a paper, you know, accepting responsibility for discharging yourself. By the way, Mr. Garrett, we have you down as no friends or relatives, and no home. That's right, isn't it?'

'Perfectly correct,' answered Ferningham calmly.

'Well — er, what are you going to do? You mustn't mind my asking,' the other added kindly, 'but have you got any money? Part of my job, you know, to ask these questions!'

'Well, to be quite candid, sir, I haven't a bean. In fact, all my worldly goods at the moment are shoes and socks, pants and vest, and a tie. My coat and shirt had to be destroyed. I gather they were rather messed up.'

'Well, why not stay on here for at any rate another week? You can't be too strong yet, you know.'

'If you don't mind, sir, I do particularly want to go tomorrow. If I can get back to Town I think I shall be all right.'

'Well, in that case,' the surgeon concluded, 'I'll let you discharge tomorrow. Come and see me in the morning. The sister will tell you when.'

Ferningham thanked him warmly and made his way back to the day ward.

The news of his discharge for the next day left the sister incredulous with astonishment. She began to expostulate with him, but finally gave it up and retreated.

That night Ferningham could hardly sleep. His brain was alive with plans for the future, and foremost amongst these was a fixed determination to trace out, if possible, the men responsible for the murder.

His mind was a seething cauldron of hate against society in general, and against the criminals in particular. Somewhere he was convinced he would find the person responsible for all this, and when he did . . . his fingers stretched yearningly, as in imagination he had the criminal in his grasp.

Meanwhile, he reflected bitterly, he was an outcast; unable to claim what was lawfully his; unable to produce any identity or references for work; nameless, except for any chance name that sprang to his lips; his real self a criminal in the eyes of the law.

So be it, he reflected with calm deliberation. Society had robbed him of his fortune, of his friends, of his station.

He would win fresh fortune, new friends, new position — and he would win it from the world. He had been preyed upon by criminals, had been plundered by society of his wealth. It would be his turn now to prey, and first he would begin on those who had been responsible. As he continued to ponder through the night, he found fresh life stealing through his veins, fresh excitement stirring his blood. His had been an orderly life and at that a trifle dull. It would be dull no longer, he promised himself.

It was nearly dawn before he slept, and when he did, it was the healthy sleep of a child.

He was up at a quarter to seven the next morning; by eight o'clock his breakfast finished, and thereafter he was condemned to fidget until nearly eleven o'clock before he was sent for discharge.

The house surgeon greeted him in a professional way. 'If you will just sign this form; thank you, Mr. Garrett. Now then, you feel quite fit? . . . Good; no aches, pains, or after-effects? . . . Good. You're quite satisfied with your treatment? . . . Good. No complaints to make in any way at all? Thank you. And you're leaving now through your own express wish? . . . Right!'

To each of the questions Ferningham had merely nodded or shaken his head. He had realised that they were purely formal ones, and were probably put to every patient leaving. The house surgeon himself hardly seemed to expect, or to wait for, any coherent answers.

Having concluded his formal enquiry, the house surgeon dropped his professional manner abruptly.

'Now, Mr. Garrett, before you go, there's just one or two things I'd like to say. Take things easily at first, won't you? You've got a magnificent constitution, I know, and a physique above the normal, but don't expect it to be up to standard for a time. Ahem! I understand that your stuff was chiefly lost in the accident, so as we're about the same size, I had an old suit of mine sent up to your ward; you'll find it there when you go back, for you to leave in, and — er — here are a few shillings from the hospital fund — er — so that you can get back to Town by train! You say you'll be all right there?'

'Quite all right, sir, and thank you very much indeed. I hope that in a short time I shall be in a position to recompense the hospital for my stay here.'

'Well, yes, I hope so, too,' the surgeon replied with a smile. 'We hospitals never say no to funds, and it will be a relief to you, I expect, when you get back to a comfortable position again. In the mean-time — er — good-bye, Mr. Garrett, and best of luck!'

Ferningham shook hands, thanked him again, and said good-bye.

He made his way back to the ward, and there found the nurse in charge of the clothes which the surgeon had so thoughtfully provided. He dressed himself with care, the fit was excellent, and, thanking his lucky stars that he had not got to appear outside in the nondescript jacket which had been loaned to him in the ward before the arrival of the suit, he made his way to the entrance hall.

The sun was shining gloriously outside as Ferningham, in his borrowed plumes, and the loan of six shillings in his trouser pocket, stopped to ask the best way back to Town. He was told that there was a frequent bus service direct to Reading Station, whence there was a good fast service to Town. Ferningham thanked the informer, an elderly workman, and was reaching in his pocket to tip the man, when he remembered the state of his finances. He flushed slightly and thanked the other warmly, hoping that the gesture had not been noticed, then he moved on to wait at the bus stop.

When the bus eventually arrived it was crowded. Ferningham was obliged to sit on the outside corner of a seat, for the rest was occupied by a market woman of gigantic proportions, who obviously worked in, or owned, a fishmonger's, for she smelt most distinctly of fish. Ferningham realised too late why others in the bus had preferred to stand. He glanced sideways at his fellow passenger and endeavoured not to wrinkle his nose at the odour. She in the meantime gazed placidly ahead of her, quite unconscious of the aura surrounding her. Beneath her old coat she wore an apron, liberally spangled with fish scales; there were even a few clinging here and there to her hard-brimmed hat.

Ferningham shuddered at the penalty that poverty was exacting from him, and prayed that the journey would not be a long one. Just as he was beginning to come to the conclusion that the journey would never end, the bus drew up in the station yard, and with a sigh of thankfulness he descended.

He made his way to the booking office, bought a third single to London, and then looked round for a telephone booth. He had resolved whilst in the bus that the first thing he would do would be to see Anne. To her at least he owed it to tell everything; as to what she would say or do, he was afraid to think; it was quite bad enough for one's fiancé to be tried and found guilty of murder; but to reappear from the dead with a totally different face would be imposing a strain which he could not expect her affection to survive. As her old aunt, who was grimly religious, would say if she knew, 'It's nothing short of blasphemous!'

He put through his call to Sloane Square, and, with a sigh, replaced his capital of fivepence in his pocket. A voice at the other end, and he pressed Button A.

'Sloane 19827? Can I speak to Miss Eversleigh, please? . . . Thank you! . . . Miss

Eversleigh? . . . My name is Garrett . . . Yes . . . No, I'm afraid you don't know me! . . . I wanted to come and see you this afternoon if I might . . . Yes, it's rather urgent. I had some confidential news about Mr. Ferningham . . . Yes — rather private. Yes — quite good news. No — don't hang up; I'm not a reporter . . . Yes — it really is important . . . Seven o'clock. Yes; thank you. Good-bye.'

He hung up the receiver and emerged wiping his forehead. It was now two o'clock and his total capital was five-pence. He decided to spend the afternoon in Reading, and found that there was a fast train leaving Reading at 6 p.m.

'Any sights worth seeing in the town?' he asked the porter.

'Well, sir, if you're fond of something quiet, there's the Forbury Gardens and Abbey Ruins round to the left. About half a mile, sir!'

'Thanks very much, that should prove exciting,' agreed Ferningham cordially, and sallied forth.

He found the Gardens without much difficulty, and after one long look he passed rapidly through.

On the further side lay the ruins, and here he breathed a sigh of relief. There were long grassy banks bathed in the afternoon sunshine, with no sign of human interest. He stretched himself on a slope and mechanically fished in his pockets for cigarettes. Even as he realised he had none, his hand encountered a square packet. He drew it out and found it to be an envelope containing twenty Players and a box of matches. The surgeon had been more than thoughtful!

He lit one, sighed luxuriously, stretched himself once or twice, and peacefully continued to smoke. Ten minutes later and he was asleep.

★   ★   ★

Minutes after, it seemed, he woke up. For a moment he could not remember where he was; then, as he stretched his stiffened limbs, he suddenly thought of the train.

He got up hurriedly, straightened his coat and looked around him.

The sun had already set, so it must be

well after five. Hastening back through the Gardens he enquired of the first person he met the time.

It was half past five. He had half an hour. He shortened his pace to a stroll, and was back on the platform by a quarter to six.

It was already dark when the six o'clock for Paddington slid slowly into the station. As it came to a standstill crowds began to pour from its entire length, for there had been racing at Newbury that afternoon. Towards the front end of the platform Ferningham rose from the bench on which he had been sitting in patient expectation of the train's arrival.

He noticed the wholesale exodus from the train with cheerful satisfaction. With any luck there should be a few empties. There were, and he climbed into one with thankfulness. 'No handbags, wallets, or old clothes left behind,' he murmured regretfully. Pity! The British racing public is definitely becoming too careful. Well, at any rate, they have left me the sole rights of this compartment, and I can now compose a treatise on 'How to Build a

Fortune on a Capital of Twopence!'

He forced himself, however, not to think of the immediate future. There was no use worrying about it, and in any case he was seeing Anne again in an hour or so, which was far more important.

Punctually at 6.50 p.m. the train crept gently into Paddington Station. Ferningham descended, feeling a trifle stiff and tired, and made his way across to the right in front of the platform entrances to the Underground.

Queensland Mansions lie within a stone's throw of Sloane Square. It was already past seven when Ferningham ascended in the lift and knocked on the door of No. 2. Now that the actual moment had arrived, he was full of nerves. His mouth was dry and his head seemed to be swimming. The maid who opened the door had opened it to him a hundred times before. He looked at her firmly, but there was not the faintest sign of recognition in her eyes.

'Mr. Garrett,' he said formally. 'I believe Miss Eversleigh is expecting me.'

'Yes, sir. If you will come this way I will

tell Miss Eversleigh you are here!'

She showed him into the drawing-room on the right of the little hall, a room which he knew only too well, and left him.

He moved aimlessly about, his heart was beating wildly; the palms of his hands were moist with nervous excitement. A photograph on a table in the far corner caught his eye. It was of himself taken some eighteen months before. He crossed over and picked it up, examining it closely. Then he moved over to a mirror on the wall, and holding the photograph alongside his face, he gazed at the reflection. The difference was even stronger than he had imagined. He heard the door open behind him, and putting down the photograph hurriedly he turned to meet the newcomer. It was Anne!

'Mr. Garrett?' she asked, wrinkling her brow slightly in a puzzled way. 'I've been waiting ever since I had your 'phone message. Won't you sit down?' She seated herself on a low slung chair on one side of the fireplace, but Ferningham did not follow her example. He was gazing at her with an odd sense of panic in his heart.

She was thinner than she had been, and her face showed signs of the strain she had undergone. Her dress was black and cut very simply. It emphasised the pallor of her neck and face, unrelieved save for the dark scarlet of her lips. Her hair was pale gold, drawn tightly down as far as the ears, with a cluster of tiny curls coming well down on to the nape of the neck.

For a moment he had an uncontrollable impulse to run away, to take her up in his arms; anything but to stand there and tell her in cold phrases what she could not see. The next he had fought it down and was already speaking.

'You heard, I suppose, of Ferningham's death, Miss — ' He could not bring himself to use the formal 'Miss Eversleigh.' She nodded dumbly. Already she had caught some of the pregnancy lying behind his words.

'Well — er — you see . . . ' But she was already on her feet before him. She gazed at him imploringly, looked at his hands mutely, gesticulating where his tongue had failed, then:

'No, no,' she cried, 'let me tell you first!

They told me Roger was dead — my Roger — but now . . . now I'll tell you, he was hurt, very badly I think . . . but he didn't die . . . he didn't! He must have been hurt, because . . . because his poor face was so altered. But they didn't alter the way he held his head,' she went on with a rush. 'They didn't alter his hands, did they? And they didn't alter him inside! *Did they* — ROGER?'

She was in his arms, crying and laughing, and he held her close to him for a long time. At length: 'I'm afraid you're in for a long speech, Roger, so before you tell me about it, I'll get you something to drink. Whisky?'

'Thanks, Anne; but just a moment,' said Roger. 'I thought I was quite safe, but you seem to have got through my disguise. What about your maid? Do you think there's any chance of her tumbling to it? I can't take any risks, my dear.'

'My dear heart,' Anne replied reassuringly, 'with the possible exception of your mother, I shouldn't think there was another person in the world who would spot you.'

'In which case,' Ferningham said with feeling, 'I'll have several drinks.'

Presently, fortified with glass and decanter, he settled down to tell her the whole story.

She was silent for a moment when he came to the end, then: 'So it means that you have got to be David Garrett from now on,' she said slowly, 'unless by some miracle the real people are discovered.'

'Exactly,' he agreed. 'And I can't touch a thing which belongs to me in the meantime.'

'And what do you propose to do, my dear? You can't go to any of your friends. The less people who know about it the better.'

'Quite! But one thing I'm going to do,' he said stubbornly. 'I'm going to get to the bottom of all this. You see, Anne,' he went on, 'that girl wasn't killed for nothing. And the way I look at it is this! If the police had not found a murderer ready to hand, they would have started enquiries into the girl's life, etc. And they would have found out something. That was why it was all arranged so nicely for me, I'm certain. Everything pointed to me, so the police didn't bother to look elsewhere; which, I think, was what the real murderer wanted. So now I'm going to look, and when I find them — well, the Lord help them!'

'*You are* going to, Roger? I think you're making a mistake,' broke in Anne with a smile that was belied by her tightly-set mouth. 'You meant to say 'we,' didn't you? Or perhaps you don't think that the last few weeks have given me any cause to be in on this?' Then, as he started to protest, she went on quickly. 'No, no, my darling, I can be very useful here, and you know it. And *I'm going* to be! In the first place, you want to find out about what the girl was doing just before her death. Well, I can help there, because I went down to see her mother only a fortnight ago. I can easily go down again now that I know her.'

'You can?' said Ferningham excitedly. 'That's splendid. But,' more slowly, 'this isn't going to be a picnic, my dear. Whoever we're up against will stop at nothing. Don't forget that! So if you — '

'That's all right, Roger. I'm tired of picnics, anyway. I'll go down and see the old lady again tomorrow, and see what I can find out. What are you going to do?'

'Well,' answered Roger thoughtfully, 'the first thing I'm going to do is to look up the porter of the flats. He'll do as well as anyone for a start, and he might know something without realising he does.'

'Then the sooner you see him the better,' Anne agreed. 'But I didn't really mean that when I asked you what you were going to do. I meant where were you going to stay and all that? It'll have to be an hotel for the present. You don't want to come here more than you can help, though I don't think you could possibly be spotted. Oh, Roger,' she broke off with a laugh, 'I'm getting used to it now, and really it's just as nice a face as the one you had before, except that you look just a wee bit grimmer, and you have lost that nice little pug nose.'

'Taking it by and large, it might have been a deal worse,' Roger agreed. 'But as regards money, I'm afraid you'll have to be my banker for the present.'

'I shall be honoured, sir,' she answered mockingly, 'but first I must make my terms clear. Whatever you do, whatever happens, *I am coming in with you.*'

Then, as he stood for a moment, she stepped very close to him, took hold of the lapels of his coat, and in a voice that trembled a little, so charged was it with purpose, she said:

'Roger, if ever you hope to see, hear, or hold me again, then don't try to keep me out of this. I suppose,' she continued reflectively, 'I was as conventional as most people. Oh, yes; I was in love with you, Roger, but in a nice, well-bred way. But — when I lost you — I think . . . I think it must have made me just a little insane. At any rate, it seemed to me that my life had been so utterly blank, so entirely futile.' She shivered a little, paused, and then went on in a low voice, 'And now you're back, Roger. Yesterday I had nothing, and today you're back. But there's this difference. Before — before it all happened we were two persons. It was all very nice, but we were still two persons. Then, when I lost you, I found I hadn't lost another person — I had lost part of myself. And now that part has come back — so there aren't two people any more. We're one person, Roger. Nothing can separate us now. Do you hear — nothing!'

He looked at her for a moment and nodded. For the life of him he couldn't have spoken just then.

'And now,' said Anne, 'I think we'll have another drink.'

6

Detective Inspector Pateman was worried . . .

Actually there should have been no reason for such a condition of mind, except for the fact that Pateman had experienced such things in the past. He was, in fact, worried because crime had fallen off. Eighteen months previously there had been a big job. In the month of December two policemen had been detailed for what was considered a soft job to assist at the collection of a quarter of a million pounds Slate Club cheque for one of London's largest Slate Clubs. The cheque had been cashed in one pound notes, ten shilling notes, silver and copper. The money had been put in a van, a policeman had got in beside the driver, and the consignment had disappeared. Two hours later the van had been found abandoned outside a London gas company's offices. One policeman had been left inside, dead, with a Christmas card bearing Yuletide greetings to the gas company. Two days later the other unfortunate policeman had been fished out of the Thames. All efforts to solve the crime had failed.

Six months had gone by, and the public had forgotten the robbery. Scotland Yard had not, although it would have liked to, since no clue had turned up. Then one afternoon a consignment of gold to the tune of £200,000 destined for the Bank of England had been stolen, somewhere between Le Bourget aerodrome and Hendon. The aeroplane had been found abandoned the next day; the pilot, a man of undoubted integrity, was not. The English Channel, however, is deep, and there was fog on the day of the flight.

At the news of this second robbery of magnitude, Scotland Yard redoubled their efforts. But the total lack of reward for their enquiries only served to emphasise the fact that somewhere in the background was a new criminal organisation, ruthlessly efficient, and already startlingly well equipped with funds.

And so the order went out. North and south they combed the country; old lags, tickets-of-leave, all the small fry of the criminal underworld, of which Scotland Yard keeps so painstaking a record, were brought in and questioned during the following few weeks. As an example of organisation it was magnificent; more than one incident served to confirm the suspicion which had been aroused.

That somewhere an organisation was moving could be felt. Here and there a guarded answer, an unexplained affluence, showed that hidden forces were afoot.

But beyond this, the police could find nothing tangible. Either the danger was too menacing, or the secret too well guarded; a few small-timers whose attitude had given rise to suspicion had been followed up, and for the time being Scotland Yard had again to confess itself baffled.

Until last Christmas!

For the previous six weeks there had been a noticeable lack of crime, ordinary or extraordinary. The respite, however, was not unwelcome, for the police had had their hands full in other directions. Despite a distinct improvement in trade generally and in the unemployment figures in particular, November and December had been remarkable for political agitation. A strike here, a riot there, hunger marches organised nearly every week and demonstrations galore had required all the tact of the police to handle. On four separate occasions there had been bloodshed, and in each instance the arrests made had brought to light only a few obvious dupes. The real agents provocateurs were obviously well hidden in the rear.

Then one Monday morning came a new bombshell! The Provincial Union Insurance Company had been robbed, again the loot was gold, this time to the tune of £300,000.

Now it is not usual for an insurance company to carry large supplies of gold in the ordinary course of business. In this case the Provincial Bank, one of England's largest insurance houses, had just completed a big business deal with a Foreign Power.

It had been in the form of a cover for

shipping, the premium had been a large one, as the international relations of the Foreign Power with its neighbours were, to say the least of it, strained: and war was a factor to be taken into account.

In addition, and partly as a result of those relations, the foreign exchange between England and the country in question was fluctuating, and the Provincial Union had therefore stipulated payment in gold.

The consignment had arrived on Saturday afternoon, the boat bringing the gold being seven hours late owing to engine trouble. The bullion, on arrival at the London Docks, had been transferred in safety to the Insurance Company's vaults. On Monday morning it was gone!

Curiously enough, although the actual insurance deal had been known to Lloyds in general, since, naturally enough, the Provincial Union had not cared to carry the whole of the insurance risk, but had let out the greater part to other companies, yet the actual method of payment had been known to very few. This was all the more curious, because the bullion had originally been intended to be transferred to the Company's bankers, to be held over the weekend for the Monday market.

And yet the thieves had made what proved to be completely successful arrangements to cope with the altered plans for the disposal of the bullion over the weekend.

'Which shows,' Inspector Pateman had declared at a conference of his superiors on Monday evening, 'they're either magicians, or else they knew of the altered plans. Which points to someone in the Insurance Company.'

For the next month, therefore, the unfortunate staff had been subjected to the most rigorous watching and questioning, but entirely without result. By now the series of robberies had reached such a prominent position in the affairs of Scotland Yard that the Press had been called into conference.

The gist of the conference had never reached the outside world, but it was significant that every paper made haste to drop the subject, referring to it only in the most guarded terms, and at ever-increasing intervals. In short, the Press was co-operating with the police.

And now, nearly six months later, there was again occurring that lull in crime which accounted for Detective Inspector Pateman's worry. As a result, he was not too pleased when his assistant brought him a card bearing the name of Anne Eversleigh. He was just on the point of telling his assistant that he was engaged when the other man, without a word, took the card from the inspector's hand and turned it over.

On the back was scribbled in pencil, 'With reference to the Kensington murder.'

Pateman looked at it with renewed interest, for this had been his case. He murmured to himself, then with a sigh said, 'Send her in.'

Anne had been waiting in another room for about twenty minutes. The plan of campaign which she and Roger had decided on between them was not an easy one. In short, it was to try to reawaken the inspector's interest in the case, to find out if the police had any information of which they knew nothing, yet at the same time not to let the police suspect that Ferningham was anything but the victim of the Great Western smash.

As she was shown into the room her first impression was one of disappointment. Pateman looked very far from being an alert inspector. He looked, in fact, an ordinary middle-aged business man, with a tendency to heaviness. She reflected bitterly that she could well understand why the police did not look farther in their search for a victim than the obvious one ready to hand.

'Good morning, Miss Eversleigh. I'm afraid I can only give you about ten minutes, so perhaps you would let me know what it is you want.'

'That's quite easy,' said Anne, sitting down. 'The trouble is whether you will be able to do it. What I want is the proof that my late fiancé, Mr. Ferningham, was innocent of the murder for which he was convicted.'

Pateman's eyebrows rose very slightly. 'I am very sorry,' he murmured conventionally, 'I had no idea you were connected.' He sat looking at his desk for a moment; then,

'Excuse me asking, but have you any information which might help? . . . '

'Inspector Pateman, I have only got what to me is the most obvious knowledge. Roger could not have done it.'

'Just a moment, if you'll excuse me,' and as he spoke Pateman pressed the dictaphone switch. 'Yes, sir,' came from the instrument on the desk.

'Fetch me the Kensington file, will you?' He turned back the switch and waved his hand to Anne to continue.

'Do you ever look at crime from anything but the obvious angle?' asked Anne.

'Quite often,' with a smile.

'Then haven't you thought that this was a little too obvious? Roger was found with a gun in his hand by your men a minute after the murder was committed. A whole minute! I do not know much about these things, but if he had done it, surely he could have pleaded that it was unpremeditated, that he didn't know what he was doing, and that it was a case

88

of manslaughter and not murder. You see, I happen to know that he could not have been — having an affair, I suppose you would call it — with that girl. I do not expect you to know that, of course, but surely nobody would act so foolishly. If Roger had waited there for you all to have arrived, wouldn't he have admitted it? . . . '

There was a knock at the door, and in reply to Pateman's 'Come in!' the assistant brought in the Kensington file.

'Excuse me a moment,' said Pateman, and began looking through the papers. For a minute there was silence while he turned over leaf after leaf, and then he suddenly looked up.

'It was a passer-by named Bessborough who called the police,' he said slowly. 'He heard the shot from the road, apparently.'

Anne nodded.

'Mr. Bessborough apparently was employed by the Provincial Insurance, Lombard Street . . . '

'I don't know what that has to do . . . ' began Anne.

'Probably nothing, but still . . . '

Pateman fiddled with the papers for a minute. He was not looking at them, though, he was looking at the wall. Finally he said:

'I take it that you wish to re-open the case.'

Anne nodded.

For the life of her she could not have said a word just then.

'Well, Miss Eversleigh, although I cannot promise you any results, I will go through it again very carefully. We do not like mistakes here, you know. That doesn't mean to say officially I have any expectations that a mistake has been made. I think the best thing will be for you to come back in two days' time. When you come back I may want to ask you all sorts of silly things, so in the meantime I want you to think over anything and everything connected with Mr. Ferningham. When you go out, perhaps you will be good enough to leave your address with my assistant. Oh! I beg your pardon,' as he looked down at his desk, 'I have your card here, of course.'

He had stood up as he was speaking

and Anne realised that the interview was over. She shook hands and left, feeling disappointed that he had not been more explicit and wondering if her visit had been wasted.

If she had been in the office at that minute she would not have been so disappointed, for hardly had the door closed when Pateman sprang into action.

From a drawer in his desk he brought out a file. It was labelled 'Provincial Insurance Company, Lombard Street.' Next, he pulled down the dictaphone switch, asking for his assistant. 'And hurry up,' he added.

'Edwards,' he said, as his assistant came in the room. 'what was the name of the policeman who arrested Ferningham?'

'Rogers, I think, sir.'

'Good. Get on to his station and tell him to come up here immediately. You know, Edwards, we may all be lowered in rank next week.'

'What makes you say that, sir?'

'Because there's a big job coming off. I can smell it. It's six months since the Provincial Insurance was robbed. Six months before then there was the gold robbery, and six months before that there was the Slate Club affair. We're just about due for the next one, Edwards.' He thought for a minute, then went on: 'Six months ago there was one of the cleverest robberies we have ever known in connection with the Provincial Insurance, and last month we had the clumsiest murder we have ever known in Kensington, and the witness to this clumsiest murder was an employee of the Provincial Insurance.

'Doesn't mean a thing, does it, Edwards?'

Edwards shook his head, bewildered. 'Not to me, sir,' he acquiesced.

'Perhaps not; but in the meantime 'phone Kensington Division and ask them if Constable Rogers is available.'

'Yes, sir,' the clerk answered, and silently withdrew. He was back again within two minutes.

'Constable Rogers is on duty in the station at the present moment, sir,' he reported.

'Good, tell him to change into plain clothes, and report here in half an hour,' replied the inspector. For the next half hour he busied himself with the revision of all the notes of the insurance case, and when Rogers arrived he was ready.

'Good morning, Rogers,' he cheerfully greeted the somewhat nervous constable. 'I've got a special job for you today. Do you remember the Kensington murder? You do! Good. Do you remember the insurance man — Bessborough was his name — who gave evidence at the trial of hearing the shot?'

'Yes, sir.'

'Right. Well, we're going to see him today. At least — I am. He works for the Provincial Insurance, and I'm wondering if he's anything to do with the robbery there.'

'The robbery, sir?' Rogers was taken aback.

'Yes! Never mind for the present, but if he is, by the time I've finished with him, he'll be scared, and that's where you come in. You're to stay outside, and to follow him up when he comes out to lunch. Do you think you can handle it?'

'I'm sure of it, sir!' replied Rogers enthusiastically.

'In that case we'll be getting along,' and Pateman rose from his desk. He crossed over to the hatstand which stood in the corner of the room, removed from there his well-worn bowler hat, and, followed by a jubilant Rogers, he made his way downstairs and out into the street.

'By the way,' Inspector Pateman said to his companion a few minutes later as they were bowling along Whitehall in a taxi. 'You're absolutely certain that you'll recognise this man again? I don't want to start a hare if you can't follow it!'

'Yes, sir,' Rogers answered. 'I had quite a good look at him when he was giving evidence at the trial. By the way, sir, do you really think there was something wrong with the trial then?'

'I don't know, and I'm afraid to think. But I can tell you this. We've had three big robberies in eighteen months, and there's a fourth coming off in the next few weeks! I can smell it! And somehow we've got to stop it! And that's not going to be by ordinary means. They're as clever as any we've tackled, and cleverer probably than we are: they know what they are going to do; we don't! So that's why I'm going haywire on a goose-chase like this because this is the sort of thing which doesn't happen in real life, which is why I think it might happen now.

'There are seven million people in London, Rogers, and out of them all it had to be a man from the Provincial, Lombard Street, who is walking about four miles from his business and six miles from home, and so becomes the chief witness to the clumsiest and most obvious murder we've had for eight years!

'And the convicted murderer in the dock comes out with the ridiculous defence of a frame-up, with a psychic belief in a sinister organisation, which, as everyone knows, exists only in books, and which you and I know happens to be in existence at the moment.

'And the chief witness is a man from the Insurance Company which was cleaned out. Too many coincidences, and I don't like them.'

It was the longest speech that Rogers had ever heard his superior utter, and he was impressed beyond belief. If there were the least grain of truth in the other's suggestion, then the work on which they were engaged was of the most vital importance. As far as Rogers was concerned, it was his big chance, and he meant to take it.

Pateman dismissed the taxi about twenty yards short of their destination, and had a last hurried counsel with his junior.

'Don't forget, you're not to lose him until you're certain he's not doing anything funny. If nothing happens at lunch time, bump into him as he's entering the office afterwards, and ask him whom you have to see about taking out a policy. He won't be able to resist it. Even if he's a crook, he'll still sell you a policy if he can! It's a disease, insurance is, and there's no cure! Then you've got to pretend that you want to fix it up that evening; he'll either ring his wife up, and tell her to fill up the decanter in the sideboard, and cart you off to his place in the evening; or else he'll take you out for a quiet friendly talk about insurance. In any case you've got to stick to him.

'If he's got to leave you for an appointment, make sure he's followed, either by yourself or by Williams. You'll have Williams from five o'clock if you want him. Now I'll just go and sow a few seeds.'

'You can rely on me, sir, and if anything further happens, I'll be on the 'phone to you.'

'Right, Rogers,' and the inspector, turning on his heel, entered the insurance buildings.

It was by no means the first visit he had made there, and the commissionaire recognised him immediately.

'Is it the General Manager you're wanting, sir?' he asked hopefully. An escort to the office meant half a minute in the lift and another half-minute in the corridor, which would give him a chance to ask respectfully for the latest news of the robbery.

'Yes, please, Thompson, that is, if he's free.'

'Well, he wouldn't be for anybody else, sir, but if you'll step this way it will be all right.'

The commissionaire paused for a moment beside the Exchange girl's switchboard.

'General Manager's office, please, Miss!' he said.

'Your godparents didn't christen you 'Hopeful,' did they?' the girl replied without turning her head, as her fingers deftly went on engaging and disengaging plugs.

'Now don't be smart, Miss!' Thompson whispered urgently, as Pateman paused by his side.

'But I haven't a line left! You'll have to wait.'

'It's the Inspector of Police himself!'

'Oh, in that case he goes in with Fire and Ambulance!' and she disconnected a line, plugged in afresh, rang through in apparently one movement.

'General Manager's office? . . . Police inspector here, sir . . . Right . . . Thank you.'

'Send him up, Sergeant! Let's hope the G.M.'s glad to see him . . . Record Office? They cut you off . . . yes! Yes! . . . All right now . . . There you are . . . ' and she reconnected the line she had disengaged.

'Better than having an ambulance call,

anyway!' Pateman chuckled over the girl's shoulder.

The telephonist turned scarlet. 'Awfully sorry!' she said. 'Mustn't mind me.'

'Fourteen days contempt of court!' and still chuckling, for he rarely made a sally, Pateman followed the sergeant to the lift. As the doors clanged,

'There'll be no more news yet about the robbery, sir?' Thompson asked hopefully.

'There's never any news, Sergeant, until the jury says 'Guilty.''

'No, sir,' the sergeant agreed doubtfully, 'yet 'tis not too comfortable for us staff, you know, sir.'

'You're not the only ones,' Pateman said thoughtfully as he remembered certain newspaper headlines regarding the police efficiency.

They left the lift on the second floor and proceeded to the General Manager's office. Thompson knocked and stepped aside for the inspector to go in. The General Manager, who was seated behind an enormous leather-topped table, rose at their entry.

'Good morning, Inspector,' he said, 'very glad to see you.' Then, as the door closed behind the regretful commissionaire, 'No fresh news, I suppose?'

'Not particularly, I'm afraid, sir,' Pateman reluctantly replied. 'But if you don't mind I'd like to have another look at your staff book and have a talk to one or two of them again.'

'Certainly, Inspector; only too pleased. Where would you like to see them? You could have them here if you like. I shall be away for a few minutes,' he concluded tactfully.

'Thank you very much. That will do nicely.'

'Here's the Staff Index,' went on the other, opening a drawer behind him. 'Each man's card has his record. Length of service, references when engaged and reports on his work and general character. Needless to say, they are . . . um . . . very confidential, Inspector.'

'Why, that should help quite a lot,' Pateman assented gratefully.

He took the drawer of cards and placed it on the corner of the table. It was surprisingly heavy. In an apparently haphazard manner he flicked them over. In reality he was looking for Bessborough's card, and the next moment he found it.

'Now this is the sort of person I want to see,' he said, with seeming indifference. 'Been here only eighteen months. Let's see — what's the name? . . . Bessborough . . . I'll just pick out a few like this and see them, if I may, sir!'

'Certainly, Inspector. I'll have Bessborough up while you are looking through the others.' He rang the bell.

'Ask Mr. Bessborough to come up, Miss Harlow, please,' he said to his secretary, 'and anyone else that this gentleman would like to see. I shall be over in the Records Office,' he went on, turning to the inspector, 'if you want me at all.'

'Thank you very much, sir,' Pateman replied, and as the door closed behind the other man he settled himself with deliberation in the opulent swivel chair behind the desk.

He had not long to wait. There was a

knock at the door, and in reply to his 'Come in!' a man of about thirty entered.

'Mr. Bessborough?' the inspector queried. 'Ah! Good morning. Take a seat.'

The other sat down, frankly bewildered. It was obvious that he had expected to find the General Manager there, and was even now wondering who the stranger might be. Pateman was silent for a minute, giving the other man time to become even more uncomfortable.

At last, 'I'm from the police, Mr. Bessborough,' he said, and watched for the reaction.

That Bessborough was startled was obvious. He flushed, and then as suddenly grew pale, while his fingers clenched and unclenched themselves. But that was not much to go upon, the inspector reflected, for any perfectly innocent person might equally well be discomforted in a like position.

He therefore continued in a reassuring voice. 'We're still collecting information regarding the robbery, and as a matter of form we have to have particulars of the staff for the last three years.'

Bessborough sat back in his chair with ill-concealed relief.

'I understand, sir. I've been here about eighteen months, I think. I was abroad for about three years before that, sir, private secretary to a gentleman. I don't know if you would like his address. It was a Mr. Hereford, 53, Nevin Square. At least, that was his address about a year ago. He was kind enough to give me a very good reference here, and as I had started in insurance when I was eighteen, they took me on.'

'I see,' said the inspector, breaking in. 'By the way, your face seems familiar. Weren't you a witness in that Kensington murder trial a few weeks ago?'

'Yes — er — yes . . . ' Bessborough's growing confidence was suddenly checked. His original nervousness was again evident.

'Unpleasant business, that,' the other went on, seemingly unconscious of the insurance clerk's embarrassment. 'Quite a coincidence that you were on the spot. So far from home and — er — work!' The question behind the statement could hardly be ignored.

'Oh! yes, yes; though I'm often down that way . . . got some friends live down there, and — er — there's a pub down there I'm very fond of . . . you know, nice and quiet, good beer, and . . . '

'Ah! yes, I see,' the inspector interjected smoothly. 'It's worth while going out of one's way to find a really comfortable pub these days. I must say it happens to be one of my weaknesses. What beer is yours?'

'What . . . ? Oh, very good beer, very . . . Oh! I see you mean what kind?'

There was no doubt now of Bessborough's panic, and the inspector felt a curious thrill, as though he were a fisherman and had seen his float move slightly.

'Let me see . . . ' the other went on unhappily, as the inspector remained silent. 'I really don't know what beer it is . . . I don't take much notice of the brand, you know, as long as it suits my stomach . . . '

'Oh! well, beer or no beer, it was lucky that you happened to be on the spot at the actual moment. By the way, you didn't see the other man come away, did you?'

'The other man? . . . I . . . I . . . ' The other's panic was barely restrained. 'No, I didn't see him. I never saw him at all.' He made an effort and forced himself to speak calmly. Only the pallor of his face and the drawn lines round his nostrils showed anything of the turmoil within.

'Is this some new evidence, sir? I didn't know there was any other man there.'

'Don't be alarmed,' said the inspector significantly. 'I was referring to the convicted man. Still, never mind. I think that's all I wanted to say. I hope you won't be so unfortunate as to be involved in any other tragedies. Good morning.'

With but badly concealed eagerness Bessborough made his escape, and Pateman leant back in his chair. If his suspicions were in any way justified, then something should come of the interview. If ever a man had seemed rattled, Bessborough had. Anyway, Rogers should be able to deal with him.

★   ★   ★

At that precise moment Rogers, who was now apparently held fascinated by a display of pale green shirts, was wondering how much longer he would be waiting there. Already he had exhausted most of the shop windows near-by, and none of them were displaying men's things, unless one counted the green shirts, which was a terrible thought . . .

In a minute, however, his patience was rewarded, as, from the corner of his eye, he saw Bessborough hurrying down the steps of the insurance buildings.

Fifty yards down the road, the other's destination became plain; it was a public telephone box. Rogers slackened pace as his quarry went inside, and stopped to examine some umbrellas in a shop near-by. He would have given worlds to have heard the man's conversation, but he consoled himself with the thought that Bessborough would probably think it too dangerous to say much on the 'phone; that was if the whole thing were not a wild goose chase. He would get the 'phone number somehow, however! He carefully noted the time of call and waited. In another two minutes he saw Bessborough replace the receiver. Immediately he started to walk to the box, and arrived there just as the other emerged. The latter mechanically held the door open, and Rogers stepped inside. There was no time to ring the Exchange; but hurriedly he jotted down the number of the call box, then turned to see if Bessborough were watching. The latter, however, was already twenty yards away, and walking quickly. Rogers took up the chase again, to see Bessborough board a No. 11 bus, travelling west. He broke into a run and managed to catch it with a final spring. Bessborough was already on top, and with a sigh of relief Rogers managed to get the side seat just inside and under the stairs, whence he would be able to see his quarry alight.

Down the Strand the bus thundered, the road being miraculously free from congestion. As, however, it narrowed by Charing Cross Station, a jam in the traffic caused it to halt abruptly. At the same moment Bessborough appeared for a moment on the platform of the bus, then jumped off.

Rogers hurried after him. For one second he had visions of his quarry catching a boat train; the next moment Bessborough had walked past the entrance to the station and had turned into the Strand Corner House.

Rogers followed him in. It was vital to get a table next to the other, but he must not arouse any possible suspicion.

The table chosen by the other man was by the window. For a moment Rogers hesitated, then, as nonchalantly as possible, he sauntered to the next table, where three elderly females sat in earnest conclave. He took the fourth chair, with his back half turned to Bessborough, and ignored the outraged looks of the other three, and proceeded to study the man.

He had not long to wait. He had just finished giving his order to the waiter, with instructions that he was to leave the bill when he brought the order, when he was conscious of a short man threading his way through the tables, obviously looking for someone. For a moment his eyes met Rogers'; then, as their gaze passed on beyond, Rogers could see them light up momentarily in recognition.

The stranger squashed past the three elderly females and settled himself at Bessborough's table.

For half a minute there was silence, then, 'Thank you for the telephone call. It is such pleasure to be able to come and see you,' the stranger said.

There was a muttered reply from Bessborough which Rogers could not catch. Again the stranger was speaking very politely, yet with a subtle manner.

'But, of course, this is an ideal place for a discussion, and it must be so very urgent, or you would not have remembered that particular telephone number.'

Rogers could feel rather than actually see Bessborough's growing discomfort. Again he could not catch what the latter answered. Vaguely he could hear odd words ...references...Kensington...pub...other man ... unfortunate coincidence. While the muttered monologue had continued, the stranger had sat at the table in silence.

At the close Rogers could hear him move in his chair as though leaning forward.

'My friend, your nerves must be very overstrung if you let little things like that worry you. I'm sure you wouldn't like me to have to prescribe for you, would you? A holiday of — fourteen years, say — would build you up, but might grow a little monotonous. Go back now, and try to remember that in business, real business, you have to keep very calm. Otherwise your health might suffer.'

Once more Bessborough replied in inaudible though frankly agitated tones. Strain as he might, Rogers could catch no more. Then suddenly, out of the corner of his eye, he saw the insurance man rise from his chair, and without any farewell make his way to the lift.

For a second Rogers was in a quandary; then, as he reflected that Bessborough was probably going straight back to the office, he decided to wait for the stranger. He sat back, therefore, prepared to spend as much time as needed over his coffee, when suddenly a voice from behind said:

'I wonder if you could oblige me with a light?' And he turned to find the stranger addressing him.

110

'Certainly,' he replied, and fished in his pockets for matches.

'Thank you so much,' answered the stranger, and having struck a match he turned back to his own food. Rogers felt his heart beating swiftly. Had anything else lain behind the stranger's request for a match? Had he been wanting to get a good look at him? That something was wrong, was afoot, he now felt certain, and, given a fair deal, he should learn something in the next few hours. The most important thing to do was to find out the stranger's identity. It would not be too easy to follow the man after the match episode, but he would merely have to trust to luck.

He sat back again and ordered another coffee, asking for his bill at the same time to be in readiness for a quick exit. He had not long to wait, for presently out of the corner of his eye he observed the stranger leave his place and make his way to the cash desk. As unconcernedly as possible he followed in the other's wake to see him mount a No. 24 bus bound for Pimlico.

There was no time for delay, for the

bus was already moving off from South Africa House to cut across down Whitehall. The stranger had already reached the top of the stairs when Rogers swung himself aboard, but, even so, the latter had an uneasy feeling that the other had looked down at the last moment.

He chose a seat in front immediately behind the driver, where he could keep an eye on the bus step in the reflection of the glass which was shadowed by the driver's back. Down Whitehall the bus made its way and through into Victoria Street. As it pulled up at the Army and Navy Stores Rogers kept an especial look-out, but there was no sign of his quarry. At Victoria Station, too, he watched carefully for any sign of the other, but again he was disappointed. A sudden panic seized him as he thought for a moment that he had missed the other descending, but almost immediately he decided that this was not so. There remained, however, a fresh problem, namely, that they were within three stops of the terminus, and he was about to leave the bus when the stranger alighted at Warwick Street, and, with

Rogers on his heels, proceeded to make his way along the Pimlico side streets.

Rogers was just rounding the third corner, when he came to a full stop. The stranger was entering a house!

He paused for a minute in reflection. Since the other had a key, he quite obviously lived there, or at any rate had a room. Half a minute was spent in indecision, then Rogers went forward, his mind made up. At the next house he stopped and rang the bell. There was no immediate answer, though a wireless continued to blare from an upstairs room.

The house was obviously one of those unsavoury ones let out in bed-sitting-rooms to all and sundry. As far as he could see, the next one was identical. Again he pressed the apology for a bell, and again waited in vain for a reply.

The landlady apparently was out, and the tenants were either too lazy to answer, or suspicious of creditors. Obviously, he would not be able to glean any information about the next door house. His alternative plan was more hazardous, namely, to ring at the house itself. On second thoughts, however, he decided that it was unlikely that the man himself would answer the door.

Accordingly he made his way down the one flight and back up the next flight of stairs, and with some misgivings pressed the lowest bell of all. There was a minute's delay and the door opened to reveal a woman of indeterminate age and distinctly unsavoury clothes.

'What is it?' she asked in an uncompromising voice.

'I'm from the Censor,' Rogers hastened to explain. 'I just want the numbers of tenants you have, and their names. They will receive the printed forms to fill in in a few days.' As he spoke he produced a notebook, and fervently hoped that she did not know the method by which a census was taken.

'Will you wait a minute?' the woman said, and without waiting for his reply she shut the door. Rogers stood there, feeling distinctly foolish, and not a little nervous. He was just wondering if it would be safer to beat a retreat, when the door again opened. 'I had left something on the gas,' the woman said, more as a statement than as any explanation for her previous rudeness. 'Come in, please.'

Rogers obeyed, still with the feeling of disquiet, and as he did so, the woman closed the door behind him. At the same moment the door of the front sitting-room opened and a man stepped into the hall. It was the stranger. 'Good after-noon,' he said very quietly. 'Doubtless you have brought me another match!'

Rogers stood there silent, unable to speak for the moment, then, as the realisation of the trap penetrated to his brain, he turned to escape. It was the last conscious movement he made. A searing pain shot through his skull. For half a second he saw the hall, the drab figure of the landlady, and the stranger with his menacing smile, in a light clearer and stronger than any light of day. Then he sagged suddenly and crumpled up on the floor.

The man who had been concealed by the opening of the door bent over the hapless Rogers. A piece of lead piping in his hand was revealed as the weapon he had just used. He looked across at the stranger. 'Is he dead?' the latter asked.

'Don't think so,' the assailant replied. 'I couldn't hit too hard; afraid of making a mess!'

'In that case . . . ' and a wave of the hand completed the sentence.

With indescribable callousness the other man bent lower over the victim, seized him by the hair and lifted his head and shoulders clear of the ground. His right hand holding the lead piping went back, and with the utmost deliberation he struck twice on the back of the neck. The body quivered dreadfully for several seconds and was still.

'O.K. now,' he said, releasing his hold and straightening up.

'Put him in the room and have him wrapped up in the carpet. I'll have the carpet collected later,' ordered the stranger as he lit a cigarette.

7

Having left Scotland Yard, Anne proceeded to her second duty as arranged between Roger and herself.

This was to visit the dead girl's mother again, and to learn as much as she could of the girl's work immediately prior to her death. Remembering her previous visit, when a small crowd of urchins had played hide and seek in and out of her car whilst she was inside the house, she decided to take a taxi. The journey was a long one, for her destination was in the wilds of Tooting. She dismissed the taxi in the next road, preferring to finish her journey on foot. The road was a squalid one. At the further end a game of football was in progress, a large saloon car being used for the only goal. Anne was thankful she had not brought her own car. As she neared the house, she was surprised to find that the car was drawn up outside it. She slackened pace for a moment. Evidently the woman had visitors and impressive ones at that. The next minute, however, the door was seen to open and a short man stepped out, followed by the girl's mother. Although the day was warm, he wore an enormous overcoat which nearly reached his ankles, a coat which was definitely not of English cut. A cigarette hung from his full lips, and although he smiled at that moment in farewell, Anne, who was by now only twelve yards away, felt a shiver run through her at the expression on his face. He was bending down to his chauffeur as she drew abreast, and although she was not paying particular attention she heard him say, 'twenty-nine, Chadworth Street,' to the driver. The next moment he had got in. Anne, with instinctive caution, walked up past the house until she heard the car move away, then, as if she had just noticed the numbers, she retraced her steps, and arrived at the door just as the woman was closing it.

'Good morning, Mrs. Webb,' Anne began, with an attempt at warmth.

'Good morning, Miss — why, it's Miss

Eversleigh.' The woman expanded as she remembered Anne's previous visit and the cheque which had accompanied it. 'Do come in, Miss Eversleigh.' Her manner changed abruptly as she remembered Anne's open purse. She heaved a sigh, appropriate for one in deep mourning, and her black dress rustled significantly.

'Come into the front room, do ... Though it's little need I should be having of this room now!' She sniffed violently, and cast despairing glances around the room in question. Anne did, too, but from a different reason. The room was typical of its kind. A dingy collection of dried grasses stood uncertainly in a hideous vase in the fireplace. Two so-called easy chairs flanked a massive brass curb, and a companion sofa stood along the wall. The room reeked of the pungent smell of American cloth. There were photographs everywhere; arranged in rows upon the mantelpiece, huddled in groups upon two bamboo tables. Cheap Nottingham lace curtains hung dustily before the bay window, mercifully obscuring the light which sought to expose the ugly secrets of the room.

'Well,' said Mrs. Webb, seating herself heavily on the sofa and motioning Anne to the chair opposite; 'I expect you've come to see how I'm getting on. Ah, dear, I 'ope it won't be long now before I'm took, there's nothing much left for me, I'm sure.' She sighed in an ecstasy of unhappiness.

'Well, Mrs. Webb, I felt that I had to come along and see how you were getting on. I was so afraid that with the loss of your daughter's income . . . '

'Yes, I'm sure I never realised until now how much I depended upon her weekly wage. You see, it is not as though she had ever had a father' (she spoke as though the union had been a heavenly one), 'and I'm sure the years I've spent bringing up my girl, and for what? For what, Miss Eversleigh? To be killed, begging yer pardon, in such a cruel way! It's not the money only, but . . . '

'Well, Mrs. Webb, that's exactly why I'm here; and you mustn't mind my trying to help you.' As she spoke, Anne hunted in her bag, and with a deft movement slipped a small wad of notes over to the eager hands of the widow. She was surprised, however, to find that their total amount was accepted almost nonchalantly by Mrs. Webb.

'Thank you very kindly, I'm sure, Miss Eversleigh,' said the widow, counting the twenty pounds surreptitiously, 'this will help me over the next few days.' She seemed to be struggling with herself for a minute, but at last burst forth with a — 'I don't know whether you saw a gentleman leave the house just before you came, Miss . . . You did? Ah, that was the manager of the Waste Paper Factory where my girl used to work. And what do you think he brought me, Miss? A cheque! And for £500.' Anne's twenty pounds wilted almost to nothing before the mention of such a sum.

'Your daughter must have held a very responsible position in this — waste paper factory, did you say, Mrs. Webb?'

'Ah,' said the latter, with every sign of satisfaction, 'she was a good gal, was Rosie!' The inference to be derived from her manner was that the girl's goodness had lain in providing such satisfactory financial connections. A form of insurance, Anne could not help thinking. 'Her job was important all right. Got introduced there by her gentleman friend. Yes, she was a clever girl.'

As to whether the cleverness lay in getting the introduction or in her actual work, the mother did not explain. Anne awakened to interest. This was what she had come for, for what she had sacrificed the twenty pounds.

'What firm was it she was working for, Mrs. Webb?' she asked bluntly.

'A waste paper firm, Miss — here, I've got the address somewhere, in case you ever want to sell any paper.' She fumbled in her bag as she spoke. Anne repressed an impulse to laugh.

'Thank you, Mrs. Webb, that may be very useful.'

'You're welcome, Miss. Ah, here it is!' She passed over a grimy envelope as though it were the most precious thing in the world. 'Huge firm it is,' she added, in blissful ignorance as to what size it actually might be.

'And you should have seen poor Rosie's gentleman friend, what was working there. American he was — wore such a lovely tiepin, all diamonds; and his ring, too, that was a diamond. Proper toff he was, though he made us call him Jake, and he used such funny expressions, you would have died, Miss! But he didn't mind when I used to laugh, in fact, he would smile, too, and then you could see two of his teeth shining with real gold. Miss.'

'They were going to be married, then?'

'Of course, Miss, you don't think I would sit and let my girl make herself cheap! Why, as soon as I thought it safe, like, after I had let them sit in the front room by themselves for an evening or two, I said to them both, 'Now you two,' I sez, 'if you have got an understanding, you tell me, because I have to get my dresses altered for the wedding,' and he looked at me, Miss, and asked me what the alimerny laws were like in England, so when I said that people didn't worry now about such laws, they just got married, he said, 'All right, we'll take a chance.' And then I knew, Miss, that he meant the laws about foreigners marrying English girls, which I wasn't quite sure about before.'

'It must have been a great shock to him.' Anne hesitated to broach further the subject of the murder.

'Well, that I can't rightly say, Miss.' The woman spoke reluctantly, but her love for scandal — however near home it might lie — won the day, and she continued:

'You see, to tell the truth, I 'asn't set eyes on him since, in fact, not for two days before it 'appened. Rosie hadn't been well, she was that nervous the last day or two, like it might have been a warning from heaven, it might. I think she must have got a fright somewhere, perhaps that traffic in the City upset her, and then, to cap it, she has a row with her gentleman — proper lovers' tiff it was — and she even asks me to take her right away.

'The ingratitude, you know, when I had worked myself to the bone for all those years, and then when she was in a good job, with a gentleman friend who could help me when I was getting on — she goes that hysterical, there's no holding her. Not but what, poor girl, she would have come round again, that I knew. But the gentleman I 'aven't set eyes on since. I went so far as to write to his firm the other day, to ask if he was still unwell — I guessed it could only be illness which had kept him from coming here — and it turned out to be the best thing I could have done. For that's how the head of the firm came to hear about me, and directly he heard he came over and gave me this cheque, with such a comforting speech, you never heard the like, except from a pulpit. He told me as how the friend — Jake we used to call him — had to go abroad on business, so he was here in his place. Wasn't that nice of him?'

'Yes,' Anne replied mechanically. Little as she knew of business men in general, yet she could not help wondering at the kind of business where the head presented cheques of £500, paying personal visits to do so. However, Roger would be the best judge of that, and feeling that at any rate her visit had not been in vain, she decided it was time to go.

'Good-bye, Miss Eversleigh, and thank you kindly, I'm sure. They say we never find our friends until trouble comes, and I'm sure you'll find yours. I don't forget, though I may seem to, that you are in trouble too, Miss Eversleigh, and though I can't help you, it is not for lack of wanting to!'

The surprising sincerity in the woman's voice touched Anne, and she felt a sudden warmth towards the other. 'Thank you,' she said abruptly, 'I'll come again some time.' and meant it. Nevertheless, it was with a feeling of relief that she got outside, and hailing a taxi, was soon on her way to meet Roger for a two o'clock lunch.

Ferningham in the meantime had had an equally busy morning. His first hour had been spent in shops. Suits, socks, ties, shirts — he had had to buy a complete outfit, but by ten o'clock he once more felt decently clad.

There was one other shop he visited which did not deal in clothes. When he came out, he had a couple of automatics and ammunition.

His next destination was Blackwater Mansions, Kensington. As he gave the address to the taxi-driver, he reflected grimly on the hundreds of other occasions he had given the same address before he had been plunged into this maelstrom of events.

He was feeling very excited, not that he had any fear of recognition there, but at the hope of what he might learn.

For he was going to interview Biggs, the porter.

Biggs, he remembered, had been away from his post on the night of the crime. This might have been a coincidence, and Biggs might know nothing. On the other hand, he might know a lot.

There was a disappointment awaiting him. The commissionaire's uniform was the same, but the face was different. He questioned the new man briefly.

'Biggs, sir?' said the other. 'No, sir, 'e's been left some time.' Ferningham passed over a couple of half-crowns with a further question.

'Well, as a matter of fact, sir, he was

sacked. That time they had the murder here, he was absent without leave. I've got his address here, sir, if you wanted it.'

'Thanks very much,' said Ferningham. Then, as he copied it down, 'Very lucky of you to have it handy,' he added.

'Well, it's a funny thing, sir, but I wouldn't have had it with me, if someone else hadn't been wanting it yesterday.'

'Somebody else?'

'Yes, sir, a lady came round here yesterday evening about seven. Waited half an hour or more, while I was getting it for her. Said she had to have it.'

'H'm, I see. Well, thank you very much,' and Ferningham turned away in search of another taxi.

He could not tell why, but he felt uneasy. Somebody else besides himself wanted to see Biggs urgently. There might be a hundred reasons, of course, for Biggs' sudden popularity.

As to what line he himself intended to pursue with the ex-porter, he was not sure. He had known him for several years and had a high regard for him, and he had more than a suspicion that Biggs would prove a staunch ally.

He had, however, made his decision by the time that the taxi finally drew up at the address. He would proceed carefully at first as one who was interested in getting the innocence of Roger Ferningham proved. From the subsequent reaction of the porter, he would then have to decide whether or not to reveal himself.

He paid off the taxi, and mounting the steps leading to the bleak-looking house which was his destination, he surveyed ruefully the three or four bells which were on each side of the door.

A total lack of inscription left him in doubt as to the right one. He chose the top left, and pressed, but there was no reply. After waiting for two minutes without any response, he renewed his attack. This time he pressed two at once.

There was still no answer, nor could he hear the bell ringing. In final desperation he pressed every bell he could see, but a continued lack of response brought him to the conclusion that the bells had long since given up the ghost.

He recommenced, therefore, on the

letter box, and almost immediately steps sounded in the hall. There was a sound of heavy breathing on the other side, plainly audible through the letter box, then the door opened and Ferningham was confronted by an outsize in London landladies.

'Good morning,' said Ferningham, raising his hat.

'Not today, thank you,' said the large lady with feeling, and slammed the door.

Ferningham renewed his attack on the letter box, and the door was opened once more.

'I'm not a canvasser or a salesman,' he began, 'I've come about a tenant of yours.'

'Oh, I'm sorry,' she answered cheerfully, 'but it was your raising your hat that made me think . . .'

'That's all right,' smiled Ferningham, 'it was about Mr. Biggs.'

'Come in, then,' broke in the landlady, her cheerfulness gone in an instant. Ferningham stepped into the hall, then turned in amazement as he heard the key grating in the lock, to see the landlady face him, back to the door, and her massive arms folded across her bosom.

'And now, before I send for the police, you can tell me what you have done with him,' she declaimed in a voice redolent of Henry Irving.

'Done with him?' queried Ferningham in helpless astonishment.

'That was what I said.'

'Well, you're making a big mistake, I'm afraid. If it's Mr. Biggs you're referring to, I wanted to see him; I haven't done anything with him.'

'You want to see him?' queried the landlady, equally astonished.

'Yes,' emphasised Ferningham, 'I came to see him! I happened to meet him yesterday, and, hearing that he was out of a job, I came, thinking I might help him.'

The landlady relaxed her hostile attitude completely.

'I'm awfully sorry, I seem to be doing nothing but make mistakes over you, but the fact is, I'm nearly worried out of my life, Mr . . . '

'Garrett is my name,' supplied Ferningham. 'I'm afraid I haven't got a card on me, but . . . '

'Oh, that's all right, Mr. Garrett. I've

had too many dealings with gentlemen when I was on the stage not to know one when I see him. Not that I mean,' she went on hurriedly, 'those kind of dealings, but you know — bouquets and cards attached, and supper parties. Ah, dear, and between you and me, Mr. Garrett, if I didn't give way once, it must have been because I did several times. But there, I'm afraid I had too soft a heart really, and besides — gentlemen aren't what they were in those days; not that I'm referring to you, sir, I'm sure. And besides, perhaps it's because I'm twice what I was.'

Ferningham had been listening to her flow with a polite smile, but now, seizing the opportunity, he broke in with: 'Has anything happened to Mr. Biggs, then, Mrs . . . ?' He paused for her to fill in the name.

'Good heavens, if I'm not talking about myself, and forgetting all about him. Mrs. Benson is my name, Mr. Garrett. Come into the sitting-room, if you don't mind.'

Ferningham was not sorry to leave the gloomy hall. With due solemnity he was ushered into the front room, where a bewildering medley of furniture met his gaze. He counted at least seven chairs, there were three tables of varying sizes, a bookcase and a bed which, with the help of a faded crimson cover, masqueraded as a divan. The landlady interpreted his gaze correctly.

'Rather a lot of furniture, you'll be thinking, Mr. Garrett, but there. I'd rather have too much than too little. Well, now,' she continued, motioning him to a solid armchair, 'I'll tell you what I'm worried about.

'Last night a woman called for Mr. Biggs, asked him if he was the person who used to work in the mansions, and, if so, she'd got a job for him as night watchman, and would he come at once.

'Well, now, Mr. Garrett, there's no gainsaying I didn't like the girl, too high and mighty, she was, and besides which I had seen her somewhere before and couldn't think where, which naturally made me a bit anxious.

'But, to tell the truth, it was a job after all, and there's been precious few of them for Mr. Biggs lately, the more's the pity, so I didn't say anything. Well, as I was going to bed, it came over me like a flash where I'd seen the young woman before. It was at the Central Bank, Lombard Street, about a month ago, and that made me wonder still more. You know and I know, Mr. Garrett, that banks don't usually go engaging men like that. Still, I thought I'd wait and see. Then this morning, when I came downstairs, there was this letter on the mat!' She paused for a moment, with full dramatic emphasis, then continued:

'I opened it, and this was what it said!' She fumbled in her bag for a moment, and drew out a sheet of paper which she passed to Ferningham. He unfolded it and read the contents aloud.

'DEAR MADAM,

I am sorry to give up the room, but I find it more convenient to live nearer to my new job. I enclose the £9 I owe you, and shall be obliged if you will keep my things until I call for them.

Yours faithfully,
S. W. BIGGS.'

'Isn't it his handwriting?' asked Ferningham.

'Yes, it's his, all right,' the landlady replied with growing excitement, 'but that's about all. That letter was meant to keep me quiet. Something's happened to him, and he's been made to write it. Why? I'll tell you why! He'd never call me 'Madam,' nor would he give up his room, he wouldn't! But he was too clever for them, he was. He wanted me to know he was forced to write it, and do you know how he has? Why, this nine pounds business. He never owed me nine pounds. Four pounds and sixpence was all he owed me, counting the cup I charged him with, which, so help me, I wouldn't have done but only to make him more careful.'

'Nine pounds, eh?' queried Ferningham. 'That certainly sounds suspicious. Especially as he wouldn't be likely to have nine pounds ordinarily, would he?'

'I should think not!' said Mrs. Benson. 'Twopence was all he had, and that I know. But can't you see them, Mr. Garrett? Must keep the landlady quiet, they say, and tell him to write to me. And Mr. Biggs thinks quick, and says 'What

135

about the nine pounds I owe her? She'll be wanting it if she thinks I'm moving.' So they give him the nine pounds to keep me quiet. Quiet indeed! I'll show them! I'll find that man if I have to tear London brick from brick to do so.'

With her last words she had risen and was now pacing along the narrow space between the furniture. Ferningham, whose mind had become a seething cauldron of excitement, leapt to his feet in front of her with a — 'Mrs. Benson, you're right, and what's more, I'm the one person who knows something about this.'

He paused for a moment, weighing in his mind how much he should disclose, then went on with a —

'Biggs was a quiet, peaceable man, with no one to wish him or do him harm until this last month or two. Right? Now, Mrs. Benson, what was the start of Biggs' bad luck? I'll tell you. It was one night when a stranger stood him some drinks at the same time that a murder was being committed at the mansions where he was hall porter. No!' he broke off as Mrs. Benson rose indignantly to confront him,

'I don't mean that he knew anything about it; I mean that he was given drinks so that he would be away and SHOULD KNOW NOTHING ABOUT IT!

'A man was found guilty of murder, Mrs. Benson, but Mr. Biggs doesn't feel happy about it. He thinks that man is innocent, he worries because he was away from his post at a time when he might have been able to prove that man's innocence.

'But suppose Biggs is right, suppose someone else is the murderer; then it was an accomplice who stood Biggs drinks, and Biggs may meet him again, which would be dangerous. And when it is a case of murder, Mrs. Benson, dangerous people must be eliminated.'

'Then what are we waiting for?' demanded the landlady. 'What about the police?'

'That's no good,' interrupted Ferningham, 'if we went to the police, Biggs would be dead long before they reached him. It's a job for us! In another quarter of an hour I shall know where to start looking for them.'

At his words Mrs. Benson stood up and started to remove her overall.

'In that case, Mr. Garrett, I'm coming with you, and God help them!'

'I'm sorry,' he replied kindly, resting a hand on her shoulder, 'but that's impossible at the moment. You've got the hardest job, waiting here; but I promise you,' as he saw the look of hopelessness which crossed her face, 'if there's a chance for you to help, you shall have it.'

He buttoned his overcoat across and picked up his hat. Then very deliberately he shook her hand. 'Don't worry, Mrs. Benson, and don't go out. I may be needing you.'

'Please God you will,' she whispered, and led the way into the hall to let him out.

8

Ferningham had arranged to meet Anne in the lounge of the Westminster Hotel. She was already waiting there when he arrived, a coffee tray in front of her. He noticed with satisfaction that apart from her the lounge was deserted.

He crossed the room to her, his feet making no sound in the deep pile of the carpet. She gave a start as he reached her, then, with an excited smile, she made room for him on the wide settee.

'My dear, thank goodness you've come.'

'Good hunting?' queried Ferningham, as he noticed her suppressed excitement.

'Very, I think,' she replied slowly. 'But let's wait until the waiter has been along. Have you had any lunch, or will a drink be enough?'

'I've had nothing since breakfast, and a drink will certainly not be enough!' Ferningham countered. 'On the other hand, perhaps two drinks will help!'

He pressed a bell button in the wall.

'Three large brandies and soda, waiter!' The waiter looked doubtfully at the two of them.

Ferningham turned to Anne apologetically.

'I'm sorry; will you have a liqueur? Brandy? Right! One liqueur brandy and three large brandies and soda, waiter! Say five-minute intervals for the three.' The waiter's face showed relieved comprehension. 'Every five minutes; certainly, sir.'

The drinks were brought, and Ferningham settled down with a sigh of satisfaction to hear the other's report. Anne did not waste time.

'The girl was working at a waste paper factory in the East End,' she began. 'Apparently she got the job from a male friend. 'Such a gentleman,' was how the mother described him. 'Wore a diamond tiepin, a diamond ring, and had real gold in his teeth!''

Ferningham winced visibly at the thought. 'A scintillating specimen,' he murmured. 'Waste paper must be a profitable industry.'

'Anyway,' Anne continued, 'the girl was getting plenty of money, either from the firm or from Beau Brummel, and everyone seemed pleased until the last few days.'

'Until the last few . . . ?'

'Exactly! Something went wrong then. The mother called it a lovers' tiff!'

'She would!' breathed Ferningham ecstatically.

'Stop it!' exclaimed Anne. 'This is serious. The girl was frightened about something, and I think the mother was frightened about losing the money.'

'Which she has now!' Ferningham commented.

'Not exactly, my dear, because not five minutes before I called, the director of the company also called and gave the mother a cheque for £500 as compensation! Do company directors do that sort of thing?' she broke off to ask.

Ferningham whistled softly. 'They might do, if they had sunstroke!'

'That's what I thought, so something I heard before I went in the house may be useful.'

'Something you heard . . . ?'

'Yes. I told you the director called just before I did. Well, when I arrived there was a large car outside the house and the chauffeur was trying to clear the children away from it. Just as I came abreast a man came out of the front door, and as he got in he said '29, Chadworth Street' to the chauffeur. And that man, Roger, was the director!'

'Chadworth Street,' repeated Ferning-ham with interest. 'That may be useful. Well, let's see what we've got. The girl was in a job at apparently unusually high pay, then she gets scared — I know that because of her letter to me — then she gets murdered, and then the company hands over £500 to the mother because she starts to make enquiries. Anne, we're on the scent!' he finished excitedly. 'Now we've got to get along to both those addresses. We may find something there.

'I'll try Chadworth Street first. No, no!' as he saw her about to break in. 'You've done your bit for the moment. This is my job. If what I think is true they'll stick at nothing! This paying off the old woman shows that they don't want any interruptions just now, and I wouldn't mind betting that is why the porter has disappeared.'

Anne gave an exclamation of surprise, and Ferningham continued. 'Of course, I'd forgotten that I haven't told you about that yet!'

He briefly ran over the events of the morning and finished with a 'So you see! We don't know what's going on at either of these places, and there's no sense in both of us rushing into trouble.'

After some argument Anne gave way. At that moment the waiter appeared with the second brandy and soda.

Ferningham thanked him, then, as he was retiring, called him back. 'By the way, waiter, you don't happen to know where Chadworth Street is, do you?'

'Chadworth Street, sir? Well, there are two or three of them in London, I think, sir. The nearest one is somewhere in Pimlico, I understand, sir.' His manner implied that he considered it slightly improper to know even that much about the district.

'Ah! That's fairly handy, so I think I'll try that first. You don't happen to know anything about the street, do you?' to the waiter.

'I'm glad to say I don't, sir,' replied the latter.

'H'm, well, no use wasting time. Anne, my dear, do you think that you could wait for me here? I ought not to be an hour at the outside.'

'But if anything happens?' queried Anne anxiously.

'Well, if I'm not back in two hours, go to this address, number twenty-one, Charrington Road, and see the porter's landlady. If the porter hasn't come back, tell her to go to the police and report it all, but tell her not to mention me at all. Then, at all events, we shall have done our best for the poor chap! Now! Now!' as he saw her about to make an objection, 'take this 1932 copy of the 'Field' and relax! I shan't be long.'

He deftly switched an ancient periodical from a near-by table on to her lap, waved his hand, and strode swiftly out of the lounge.

'Taxi, sir?' the commissionaire on the steps sprang to life.

'Yes, please. Tell the driver Chadworth Street, Pimlico.'

'Pimlico! Very good, sir,' replied the commissionaire doubtfully, but saluted more cheerfully as his gloved hand met Ferningham's.

They had not gone far before Ferningham rapped on the window. The driver pulled up at the kerb enquiringly.

'I want to go to number twenty-nine, driver, but I want you to pull up round the nearest corner to it, out of sight but ready to move off.'

'Yes, sir,' said the driver cheerfully. 'Will you be bringing much luggage away, sir?'

'Luggage?' the other queried; then, with a smile, 'No, no; it's not that sort of exit, but I may be bringing something or somebody, so be ready.'

'Well, so long as it'll go in the cab,' the driver assented happily, and remounting his seat they continued on their way.

Within five minutes they had arrived at a strategic corner, and with renewed instructions Ferningham left the taxi and made his way towards number twenty-nine. He had no definite plan in his mind, preferring to trust to the inspiration of the moment. If a rough house seemed necessary, he would be the one to start it, and trust to the surprise to outweigh numbers.

He paused for a moment with his hand on the knocker, loosened the automatic in his pocket, and then knocked.

There was no reply. He knocked again, louder this time, and suddenly the door of the next house opened. He turned to see an elderly woman looking at him with helpful eagerness.

'Just gone out, sir!' she volunteered.

'Oh — er — have they?' queried Ferningham.

''Im, sir, not they! There's only been the youngest in there all day, not counting the invalid, of course.'

Ferningham had a sudden inspiration.

'Confound the fool!' he exclaimed. Then by way of explanation he went on, 'It's one of my men, you see. I told him to wait for me as I've something of importance to collect, and I want to see the invalid. Unfortunately, I have no key, and I suppose that he's got his with him. I can only afford to wait a couple of minutes, too.'

'Well, if it's only a key you want, you can 'ave mine. I 'appen to know it fits, becos Mrs. Miles wot used 'ter live there afore your people, once lent me 'er key to open my door, and it fitted. Not but what I 'ad a second lock made for my door after that, and I will say my coal 'as lasted as long again since then, even though Mrs. Miles called me a suspicious what not.'

Inwardly Ferningham blessed his luck, though outwardly he remained calm.

'That will be very good of you. It will save me a lot of trouble.'

''Ere you are then, sir, and welcome,' said the neighbour, withdrawing her key from the inside of her door. 'Don't put it in too far or it won't turn — at least,' she added hurriedly, as though to defend herself against the obvious suspicion, 'that's 'ow I 'as to use it in mine, and I expect these locks are all the same.'

Ferningham's eyes twinkled as he thought of the late Mrs. Miles.

'Well, we'll try it your way,' he said, and, stooping, he unlocked the door with little difficulty. 'Thanks very much,' he concluded. 'I shall be all right now,' and devoutly hoped he would be!

Inside the hall he paused for a moment, and gently shut the street door behind him. His brain raced as he considered the immediate problems. Speed was essential. How many minutes' or even seconds' grace had he before the man returned he knew not. First, however, it was essential to secure a line of retreat.

He glanced swiftly through the ground-floor room, noting their meagre furnishings, then made for the scullery door at the rear. As he had expected, it was locked and bolted. Carefully he freed it, and as silently as possible he crept downstairs. Two rooms were on the first floor; one was completely bare of furniture and the other contained cheap bedroom furniture with two single iron beds. Whoever used them had evidently no leanings towards comfort.

Having drawn blank so far, Ferningham paused before ascending to the second and last floor. The noises from the street below served but to intensify the silence inside. The very air seemed impregnated with a heavy odour, the odour of death.

Bracing himself, Ferningham began the final climb, his nerves tautened, and his automatic, which until now had rested in his pocket, in his right hand.

As he mounted the stairs the odour of death grew stronger. His mouth tightened as he thought of the porter, but he did not pause.

Arriving at the landing he tried the handle of the nearest door. It was locked. He crossed to the other. That was also. He turned, looking round instinctively to find some weapon with which to force the lock, when suddenly there came a muffled groan from within.

At that he cast caution to the winds. Shifting his automatic to his left hand, he turned to present his right shoulder to the door. He poised for a split second on his left leg, then hurled himself forward.

There was a splintering crash, and the door flew wide open. Ferningham's charge took him headlong into the room, but even in that mad rush he remembered to drop on one knee, lest he should prove an immediate target. The precaution was needless. The room was occupied, indeed, but its occupant was quite helpless. Upon the bed in the further corner a figure lay, bound with coil upon coil of rope, and gagged with a dirty grey cloth.

Ferningham uttered an exclamation. Two strides brought him to the bedside, and wasting no time in words, he tore at the knots of the gag.

In two seconds the cloth was free, and he drew it clear. 'Thank the Lord!' he exclaimed, for it was the porter, Biggs.

Then, with an 'All right, old man, we'll soon get rid of these,' he set to work on the ropes with the knife he had bought that morning. In a minute the job was done, and with an arm round the other, he helped him to sit up.

'How are you feeling?' he asked.

'All right in a minute, sir,' answered the porter with difficulty. The gag had done its work only too well, and his mouth and tongue were swollen and bruised. Ferningham crossed over to the washstand opposite, where stood a jug of water and a cracked tumbler. He filled the latter and brought it back.

'Here, drink this,' he said kindly. The other obeyed.

'Now then,' continued Ferningham a moment later. 'I'm sorry to rush you, but we haven't much time. Do you think you can walk, or are you still feeling the effects of the rope?'

'Pins and needles pretty bad,' grunted Briggs, 'but I should be all right in 'arf a sec.'

He rose unsteadily to his feet and stamped on the floor, cursing gently. Ferningham sighed with relief. The job would be easier now since Biggs could walk. He rapidly explained how he had got in, and how the gaoler might return at any moment. 'But before we go,' he finished, 'I want to have a look in the next room, then you can tell me all that you know when we're in the taxi.'

'Right, sir,' answered Biggs. 'I reckon we can start now,' and to prove his words he led the way to the door. Ferningham followed and together they inspected the lock to the room opposite. 'Not much to this one either,' Ferningham muttered as he stepped back a pace, raised his right foot, and with hand on the banister to steady himself, drove hard at the lock with his heel. There was a sound of splintering wood. He repeated his effort, the door sagged open and they entered together.

Biggs sniffed loudly. 'Blasted stuffy in 'ere, sir. Smells queer, too,' he remarked.

Ferningham looked round. There were two chairs, a table with a telephone on it, and in the corner a bulky roll of carpet. Even as he looked at the carpet, Ferningham remembered the odour when he first came up the stairs.

He bent over the roll and began to undo it. Two turns were enough. He straightened suddenly. A hand had come into view.

'Lumme! A stiff 'un!' gasped Biggs.

'We've got to get out of here quickly,' muttered Ferningham, staring down at the carpet. A bell shattered the moment's silence! They both whirled round. It was the telephone!

'Do you know your man's voice?' Ferningham hissed. Biggs nodded excitedly.

'Right, take the 'phone. Just say 'Hello!' If he asks any questions that you can answer with 'Yes,' just say 'Yes.' If he asks anything you don't know, say 'Who's that? What do you mean?' and pretend it's the wrong number.'

Biggs nodded and crossed over. 'Hello,' he said in a deep voice. He listened for ten seconds, then with an 'O.K.' he put the receiver down. He turned to Ferningham. 'Thought I'd better say 'O.K.,' sir. It's a favourite word of that other swine,' he explained. Then: 'He didn't ask no questions; just said, 'The van'll be calling for the carpet in a quarter of an hour. Have it ready.' 'Spose he meant that, sir . . . ' and Biggs nodded at the swathed corpse with a shudder.

'Then he went on — you know, sir, it sounded inhuman — without changing his voice, 'there'll be another carpet come in by the van, so have that rolled up too, but be careful it doesn't get stained. I'll have that collected half an hour after.

Then report at the factory at half past four, not later.'

'That was all?' queried Ferningham.

'Yessir, an' quite enough, too. If you 'adn't come in, sir — well — they won't need that other carpet now, anyway!'

'We'll have to be moving,' said Ferningham. 'The factory, eh? I think I know where that is. Well, we can't do any more here. Come along and go quietly.'

He led the way down the stairs with ears alert. Half-way down there sounded the click of the door lock. They exchanged alarmed glances. The watch-man had returned! Ferningham listened to the footsteps on the stairs.

'Only one,' he whispered. 'Leave him to me.' He retreated a step so that he was hidden by the turn, and waited. The footsteps paused, the man had reached the first-floor landing. The next moment the footsteps recommenced. One, two, three, the man had mounted the turns. Ferningham whipped round the corner stair and leapt, so that as the man raised his head at the sound, Ferningham's boots crashed into his neck and chest.

154

The lower landing was a swirl of arms and legs. Then, suddenly, as both were rising to their feet, Ferningham gave a heave. Up went the watchman against the banister, up and over!

There was a heavy thud in the hall below. Ferningham peered over, but the other lay motionless. He turned to summon Biggs, but the latter was already by his side.

'That's finished him!' Biggs muttered savagely. 'Now they'll be able ter use the other carpet,' he added with ghoulish glee.

They hastened down and bent over the man. One look was sufficient, his neck was broken. Ferningham thought quickly. He wished now that he had not asked the taxi to wait. However, it could not be helped. Together they stepped over the body and, opening the door, they passed into the street.

Turning the corner, they found the taxi was still there, and at the sight of them the driver sprang to the door.

'No hurry,' said Ferningham untruthfully, and then: 'Victoria Station.'

'Very good, sir,' replied the driver. 'Which entrance, sir — Continental or Main?'

'Main entrance, thanks,' was the reply.

Alighting from the taxi, Ferningham made his way to the telephone box inside the hall, and rang up the hotel where Anne was waiting. She was still there and in a moment her voice came over the wires.

'Listen, Anne,' said Ferningham hurriedly. 'Roger speaking. Everything's O.K., and Biggs is with me. But I can't come over to the hotel, so will you meet me at Biggs' address — you know it? Good. Oh, and don't take a taxi from the hotel . . . No . . . You understand? . . . Right. Good-bye.'

He replaced the receiver, waited a minute, inserted another twopence, and with deliberation he dialled Whitehall 1212. Then 'Hello, Scotland Yard? You'll find a dead body in Chadworth Street, Pimlico, No. 29. Also a dead gaoler in the hall . . . Good-bye.'

'Just as well to let the police pick up the dead bodies,' he argued to Biggs. 'As long as they don't trace our connection in it for the moment, I should help to put them on the trail; and if we keep an eye on the papers we should find out who the dead people are, which may help us.

'Now,' he continued, taking Biggs by the arm, 'we're off to your diggings to appease your landlady's heart. She was the first to be suspicious.' And he related his interview with Mrs. Benson.

'Ah! I thought that letter would wake her up,' Biggs replied with satisfaction. 'No flies on Ma, y'know, sir. Which way'll we go? The tube's quite handy.'

'Yes, and better for our purpose, I think,' agreed Ferningham. 'Now then, don't talk too loud, but tell me all that happened.'

'Not much to tell, sir. You've 'eard 'ow the woman called for me. Well, after we'd gone about two 'undred yards, the woman ups and says, 'I think I'll drive for a bit, Sims.' So the chauffeur says, 'Righto, Miss,' and they change places. Then a minute after, the chauffeur suddenly says, 'Good Lord, what's that?' and I turns to look out of the window, and there's a 'ell of a belt on me 'ead. An' that's all I know till just before you comes along, sir.'

'Well now, look, Biggs, you've earned a rest, and at the same time you can be useful. When we get to your place you've got to stay there, and to answer the door to nobody but myself, or the young lady who'll be waiting there. I can't explain now. I'll tell you everything when we get indoors; but this is a very big thing.'

They said no more until Charrington Road was reached. Anne was already there, and with the landlady was eagerly awaiting them.

''Ullo, Ma,' said Biggs, 'me noo job didn't last so long, you see!'

'Nor will you,' replied Mrs. Benson with fervour, 'if you don't get outside of this,' and she dragged him towards a steaming plate ready on the kitchen table. 'You don't mind, sir,' she said to Ferningham over her shoulder, 'but if he starts to talk he'll never eat his food.'

'That's all right,' smiled Ferningham. 'There'll be time to talk afterwards.'

Ten minutes later they were all seated

in Mrs. Benson's 'best room,' as she termed it, and Ferningham began.

'Well, Biggs, there's a lot of things you don't know, which I think you should know now.' And without any more ado he revealed his identity, and briefly gave his conjectured reasons for the events which had just taken place.

'So you see, Biggs, I think that in some way they regard you as a weak spot in the scheme. Heaven knows why they have become so desperate suddenly, unless there's a big thing hatching at the moment, with which the murder is connected, and which they're determined not to spoil. But what I want to make clear is that you have a perfect right to go to the police, tell them all you know, and ask for protection; and if you wish to do that, don't worry but do it. I shall understand.'

'Well, sir,' replied Biggs slowly, 'as I understand it, it's like this. If I 'adn't 'ad that drink you would never 'ave been saddled with the murder; and if I keep quiet now, there's no reason for the police ever to find out that you're alive! Added to which, there's no reason why I shouldn't keep quiet, an' at the same time lend you a 'and, which — begging your pardon, sir — you may be able to do with. So there it is. I let you down once, sir, and that was once too often. From now on, if you can give me a job, sir — well, I'm only too glad to be at work again, sir.' Then, as if to relieve the tension, he dug Mrs. Benson in the ribs and hissed, ''Ow's that, Ma?'

But for once Mrs. Benson was without words, and she mutely patted his shoulder to show she understood.

Even Ferningham found it hard to speak, so moved was he by the man's sincerity. 'Thank you, Biggs,' he said abruptly, and shook hands.

His action broke the spell. Mrs. Benson advanced with, 'And if there's anything I can do, Mr. Ferningham, should I say, I only hope you'll give me the opportunity.'

At this Anne sprang from her chair. 'Mr. Biggs,' she exclaimed, 'you're an angel, and you're another one, Mrs. Benson!'

'Well,' concluded Roger, 'I won't say that you haven't taken a load off my mind, but, anyway, we'll see this thing through together. And now,' with a more business-like tone, 'let's get down to the next job. I'm inclined to think that the solution to all this lies in that waste paper factory. It's where the girl was working just before her death; and it's probably the same factory that the man was told to report at this afternoon on the telephone; which means that I am going to have a look at it right away.

'Now, Biggs, you're going to remain here with Mrs. Benson. I shall get in touch with you within the next three or four hours, but if you haven't heard from me by seven tomorrow morning, go straight down to the factory, and when you get near there, get hold of the nearest bobby and say that you were just going by the factory when you heard voices up there as though fighting was going on. If there isn't a policeman handy, ring them up. Don't say more than that, but make it sound important enough for them to take a look round the place.'

'And what about me?' asked Anne with emphasis.

'I'm afraid you can't come breaking in with me so . . . '

'I don't see why not; but even so, can't I come along and wait fairly handy in some café? I shall be an additional link in communications, Roger, in case you're in a hurry.'

'Well,' agreed Roger reluctantly, 'that should be a good idea. Always provided that you remain a communication only. In which case,' consulting his watch, 'as it's three o'clock, we'll be getting along.'

9

The buzz of the loud-speaker dictaphone sounded and Pateman threw up the tiny switch.

'Unknown 'phone call just reported dead body lying in 29, Chadworth Street, Pimlico, sir,' sounded an impersonal voice out of the box.

''Phone call traced to the public call box, Victoria Station,' the voice continued.

'Have number three car with two men outside immediately,' Pateman broke in, and hurried down the stairs to find the car drawing level with the steps outside.

'Ambulance and number four car to follow me,' Pateman rapped out to the policeman on duty at the steps. '29, Chadworth Street, is the address. Get the office to tell B Division immediately, to inform all their men.'

The car was already moving when he swung aboard. 'You know Chadworth

Street?' he asked the driver. 'Yessir,' was the answer.

Rapidly they swung along the Embankment, came up by Westminster, leaving the Houses of Parliament on the left, and, cutting across Great Peter Street and Great Smith Street, they raced through Rochester Row. Within two and a half minutes they were in Pimlico, three and a half and they were at 29, Chadworth Street.

Pateman rang the bell of the house next door. It was opened by the same woman who had helped Roger earlier on.

'Any way into the house next door?' he enquired brusquely.

'Someone else wanting to borrow my key?' she began, then suddenly, ''Oo are you, anyway?'

'Police!' came the laconic reply. 'Have you got the key?'

The woman burst into a torrent of explanation, but was cut short.

'Never mind all that now. If your key fits, I'll have it. Jackson — ' Pateman continued, 'Go through this house and watch the back garden next door. That the key?' to the woman. 'Right! Come along, Sergeant.' Then to the woman again — 'You stay here. You can tell us all about the key later.'

'Yessir, yessir . . . ' said the scared woman. ''Aven't done nothin' with the key, sir — ,' but Pateman was already opening the door of 29.

'Anyone there?' he called out. There was no reply. He stepped in, followed by the sergeant and the second plain clothes man. At their feet lay a huddled body, its head grotesquely askew.

'Close that door!' hissed Pateman. The sergeant kicked it to.

'Whoever's up there, come down!' Pateman called again, but again there was no reply.

He bent forward to examine the body. 'Dead all right, neck's broken,' he murmured: then with a start, 'Good heavens! It's the insurance chap, Bessborough.'

It was, and for the first time Pateman felt a little happier. Somewhere in this house might be a clue to help him in his search. He turned to the plain clothes man.

'Stay here, Patterson,' he ordered. 'Sergeant, come along with me.'

Together they hurriedly inspected the ground floor, then ascended the stairs. 'Nothing here, sir,' grunted the sergeant, as he looked in the two rooms on the first floor.

'Right,' answered Pateman. 'Carefully now, though,' and they began to climb the last flight.

'Hallo, hallo,' he continued as he reached the top landing, to find the shattered doors. 'Something's happened here.' He entered the room where Biggs had been imprisoned and his attention was immediately riveted on the bed, with the severed pieces of rope. 'Take a look in the other room, Sergeant,' he said, and bent to examine the bed.

'Someone has been tied up here and then cut loose,' he murmured. 'Looks as though someone else must have done the cutting loose. Too much rope for the man to have been able to have done it himself.'

'Inspector!' It was a cry rather than a call.

Pateman hurried into the next room. The sergeant was leaning against the table, staring at the roll of carpet. The

166

inspector's gaze followed the other's; a hand was protruding from the roll!

With an oath he sprang forward, and kneeling down, he pulled at the end of the carpet. The tug may have been more vigorous than he had intended. At any rate, as though it had acquired some dreadful momentum of its own, the roll unravelled rapidly across the floor — jerkily — unevenly — until its ghastly contents came to rest with a thud at the sergeant's very feet! . . . For a moment they both stared in silence!

'Roger?' the sergeant groaned, asking a question as though to deny the inevitable answer. Pateman could only nod in reply.

There was a sound of cars drawing up outside. The inspector looked out of the window. It was number four car and the ambulance.

'Go down and send the doctor with two men up here, Sergeant, then stay downstairs and see that the crowd are kept moving.' He did not want the sergeant to remain in the room longer than was necessary.

'Yessir,' said the sergeant dully, and

with a last look at the body of his friend, he turned and left the room.

Pateman did not waste time examining the body. The doctor could do that more efficiently. He made a rapid survey of the room, noted the telephone number, searched without success for any documents, papers, or any form of writing, then left to finish his examination of the first room.

On the landing he met the doctor. 'In there,' he nodded over his shoulder. 'Just let me know, Doctor, how long he's been dead, and the cause, if you don't mind; then we'll have him taken away in the ambulance, and you can make a proper examination afterwards.'

He continued into the room he had first entered. Again, apart from the severed ropes and the discarded gag, there was nothing much to learn. He gazed for a minute at the half empty tumbler of water which Ferningham had left on the floor, and at the drips of water glistening by the bed. Here was something more definite. Carefully he lifted the tumbler, using his handkerchief to hold it, and poured away the water that was left. Then, wrapping the empty glass in the handkerchief, he put it away in his side pocket.

He sat down on the bed to puzzle things out. He had two dead men, the detective Rogers, and Bessborough the insurance man. Since Rogers had been tracking Bessborough, it was reasonable to suppose that Bessborough was on the murderer's side.

Then there were signs of a prisoner having just been set free in this room. It couldn't have happened long before, because the floor was still wet from the tumbler which had doubtless been used to revive the prisoner.

That made someone AGAINST the murderers. But it seemed obvious that there must have been a rescuer as well. And between them, whilst escaping, they had killed Bessborough.

He slapped his knee in triumph as the pattern of events became clearer. Then it was probably the escaped man and rescuer who had 'phoned Scotland Yard. Which showed that they, too, had something to hide, or they would have gone along themselves.

Probably another gang, he mused, and rose to his feet. At that moment the doctor rejoined him.

'Probably been dead two hours, Inspector,' was the report. 'Cause of death, two heavy blows with something blunt and smooth. One fractured the skull, the other broke his neck. Should say the skull blow came first.'

Pateman sighed. 'Thanks, Doctor, we'll be getting down, then.'

The group collected round the body in the hall, straightened itself as the inspector came into view.

'Not much to worry about with this chap,' commented the doctor as he knelt beside the corpse. 'H'm . . . several bruises . . . superficial . . . much scratched . . . '
He rose at length and dusted his trousers at the knees. 'Someone has had a fight with him, and then dropped him down the stairs, I should say. There's a bruise right at the back of his head, and his neck is broken quite scientifically.'

He closed his bag with a click.

'Good-bye, gentlemen,' he remarked cheerfully, then turning to the huddled form, 'No,' he said anxiously, 'Don't bother to get up, I'll see you later at the mortuary!'

Pateman smiled faintly, then, turning to the men round him, he said, 'Have the two bodies taken away now; Sergeant, keep your two men here and search the place as thoroughly as you can. Look out for all finger-prints, and any letters or papers. Ring Exchange, and tell them to send a list of all 'phone calls they can trace to and from here . . . Jackson, you go and tell that woman next door to put a hat and coat on — if she's got them — and come along in the car.'

Jackson hastened to obey. Ignoring the comments of the crowd outside, he knocked at the next door. 'If you're wanting me, 'ere I am, and 'ere I've been for the last quarter of an hour,' came a voice from the pavement behind him.

'Might have guessed you'd have been outside,' Jackson replied. 'Come along, Ma. The inspector wants to have a word with you at the station.'

"Ave I got to ride in one of them little waspy things?' she questioned, with a nod in the direction of the racing police cars. Then, as though prompted by the urgent whispering of the crowd behind her,

'Do I get any reward for givin' you information?'

'Can't promise that, Ma,' replied Jackson good-humouredly, 'but you'll probably get a light sentence.'

The crowd roared at the remark. The woman started to argue, but was cut short. Clumsily she climbed into a seat behind the driver, and sat bolt upright.

The inspector got in beside the driver, and with an acceleration that threw the woman backwards against the rear cushions, the car raced off.

At the corner it narrowly missed a van which was turning into Chadworth Street. Pateman swore at the narrowness of the escape. His language would have been very much worse if he had known that in missing the van he was missing a very valuable clue.

There were two men in the van, two men and a carpet. Already the passenger had seen the ambulance and crowd. 'Steady,' he said, laying a hand on the driver's arm. Then, 'Drive straight on,' he ordered, 'and pull up round the next corner!' The other obeyed, and the first man, descending, made his way back to the crowd.

'Excuse me — if you please!' he murmured quite gently, and it was significant of his personality that the crowd opened a little to allow him passage through. As he reached the inmost circle of spectators he paused and lit a cigarette. 'An accident, perhaps?' he asked the constable on duty sleepily.

'More than that,' was the brief answer. The man was not disconcerted by the reply. His cigarette dangling from his lip, he surveyed the door with eyes which were nearly closed. At that moment the door was opened from within, and two men carrying a stretcher made their appearance. The man regarded them quietly as they descended and crossed in front of him to the ambulance. A second stretcher followed the first.

The man from the van rolled the

cigarette between his lips and turned to the constable.

'What a pity,' he remarked. 'Their faces are covered up.'

The policeman looked at him bewildered. 'What do you mean? 'What a pity?''

'It means — they are dead,' offered the stranger. 'Doesn't it?'

'Oh — yes! I see what you mean! Couldn't understand you at first,' said the constable in explanation. 'Yes, they're dead right enough. Both of them.'

'Perhaps they had a quarrel — and killed each other?' proffered the man.

'No fear!' the constable denied vigorously. 'Our chaps wouldn't do . . .'

'So one is a policeman?' queried the other quickly, but the constable realised that he had already said more than he should.

'Anyway, you'll read about it in the morning,' he concluded a little brusquely. Then, turning to the crowd, he called out, 'Come along there, move along now.' The crowd began to disperse, and the stranger returned to the waiting van.

'What's the matter, sir?' asked the driver anxiously.

'I — don't — know!' said the other with deliberation. 'But apparently you won't be needed now. Take the van back to the garage, and then report at the factory.'

'What shall I do with the carpet, sir?'

'The carpet? . . . You can give that to your — wife!'

The man shuddered slightly. 'Thank you, sir, but . . . '

'But don't be late at the factory,' broke in the other with sudden ferocity. Then, with ominous control of voice, 'Some of you are beginning to become careless . . . By the time you get back I shall know who it is . . . Good-bye.'

Hastily the man engaged his gears and drove away. He crossed the river at Vauxhall, and made his way east towards the docks.

He pulled up at length before a row of houses in a huddled street in Rotherhithe, and sounded his horn twice. A woman appeared at one of the front doors, and seeing him at the wheel, ran up to the driver's cabin.

'You're soon back, Jim,' she said wonderingly.

'Only for a minute,' he replied. 'There's a carpet inside there. Lug it out. It's for you.'

With an exclamation of delight, the woman ran round to the back of the van, and began to struggle with the tail-board. Her husband joined her, and between them they carried the carpet into the house.

'Jim!' she exclaimed. 'What a beauty! I'll put it in our bedroom.'

'Like hell you will!' was the unexpected answer.

'Why? What's the matter? It'll go well in our bedroom.'

'Put it in the . . . Oh! put it in the front room!' he decided irritably.

'But you never use the front room, Jim.'

'That's what I meant!' came the unlooked-for answer. The woman shrugged her shoulders. Then, with a softening in her voice, 'Will you be late again tonight, Jim?'

''Spect so! Overtime work again. May carry straight into the night shift. Anyway, don't wait up.' He patted her shoulder, then suddenly bent and awkwardly kissed her.

'Look after yourself, my gel,' he said, and climbed back into the van. The woman said nothing. Her hand went up to the cheek which bore the unwonted caress, and with a strange look in her eyes she watched the van out of sight . . .

10

It was a quarter to four by the time that Roger and Anne had arrived at the factory. It formed the end of a cul-de-sac. On the ground floor was a yard with two immense doors at the entrance. There was room for the largest lorry to draw in. At the side was a small door with a flight of stairs just inside, leading apparently to offices above. There were two storeys above the yard, with four windows, fairly small and looking out over the cul-de-sac. The property was very old, with wooden beams running across and very unkempt.

'I must say it all looks very genuine,' said Anne.

'And yet, if we're on the right lines, it can only be a 'front' for the gang,' replied Roger. 'Yet, why a waste paper factory? What in the world has waste paper got to do with crime? Anyway,' he continued, 'let's find somewhere handy where we can work out the next move.'

Together they retraced their steps round the corner.

'This will do,' said Roger, stopping suddenly at the door of a small café of the 'Pull up for Carmen' type. 'Not very clean, but we can't be too fussy round here.'

He hesitated at the entrance.

'We'll just go in and have tea and sandwiches. I'll drink my tea and then say I'm going to telephone. You wait and do the best you can with the sandwiches. If I'm not back in half an hour, pay the bill and walk up and down outside for another ten minutes. Then if I haven't turned up, 'phone Scotland Yard and get that detective down here. Tell him as much as you like, then, except that I'm Ferningham. Say I'm a friend of the — er — late fiancé whom you enlisted in the search for the real criminal. But impress on him that whatever is going on is coming to a head, probably within the next twenty-four hours.'

'But what are you going to do, Roger?'

'I've got to get into that factory. There's nothing else for it. If there's anyone there, as there will be for certain, I shall say that I'm interested in buying the site. Most of the property in that block is up for sale, so it's quite a reasonable suggestion, and I shall just be an agent negotiating for the whole block. Now we'll go in and get our tea.'

There were three customers inside. Two of them were playing the pin table at the far end, the other was drinking tea. All of them looked with hard suspicious eyes at the strangers as they entered.

The man behind the counter was swabbing with a damp cloth. He did not seem too pleased at the extra custom, either.

'Two teas and sandwiches,' asked Roger.

'No sandwiches.'

'What have you got, then?'

'Ham rolls,' said the other briefly.

Roger raised his eyes at Anne, who nodded. 'They'll do,' she said.

'Do you know anything about the factory round the corner? Waste paper place, isn't it?' asked Roger, as the tea and rolls were brought to them.

'Not a thing,' was the reply. 'Why? Have you some waste paper to sell?'

'No. I am interested in buying property and I wondered if the factory was working or whether it could be bought.'

The café proprietor looked at him for a moment as if he were going to say something, but appeared to change his mind and returned to his corner in silence. Obviously, he was not to be drawn into any discussion on the factory business. Roger finished his tea in two long draughts and then, turning to Anne and raising his voice slightly, he said:

'I think I'll just go and 'phone, my dear, while you're finishing your rolls.'

Anne appeared unconcerned as he left the café, though inwardly she felt far from easy. To calm her apprehension she picked up the evening paper which was lying near-by on a table and tried to interest herself in its contents. In spite of it, however, she could sense that the atmosphere in the café was far from well. There was no sound from the pin table now, and she could feel that all the occupants were watching her. She would have given a lot to have been able to pay her bill and walk out, but she tried to reassure herself with the fact that her job was far easier than Roger's.

There was the sound of footsteps behind her. They stopped at her table.

'Have you got the 2.30 results there, Miss?' a voice asked.

'The 2.30 results . . . Oh! you mean the racing results,' she replied. 'You can look at the paper if you like.' She passed the paper over.

'Thanks,' said the man and deliberately sat down opposite her.

Immediately she had handed over the paper Anne knew she should not have done it, for she had given up her protection against conversation.

She started to look in her handbag for something with which to busy herself, but as she did so the man began to speak.

'Stranger to these parts, Miss, aren't you?'

'Why — er — yes. I don't know these parts very well.'

'Boy friend left you here?' was the next question crudely delivered.

'If you mean the man who was with me, he has gone to look at some property he is thinking of buying at the corner of the street. But I expect he'll be back soon,' she could not help adding.

'Funny place to leave you,' the man volunteered suspiciously.

'Have you finished looking at your racing results?' Anne parried.

'Thanks,' he replied. 'I know them.'

Her pulse was racing now, but she kept a calm face.

'In that case I'll have my paper back,' she announced, taking it from his hands.

He seemed disconcerted by her action and uncertain as to what to do or say next. Then with a shrug he got up and crossed over to the counter. Anne could hear a whispered conversation. Then, without looking, she heard him cross to the door. There followed the clang of the bell announcing his exit, and she sighed with relief.

In the meantime Roger had made his way to the cul-de-sac. As he crossed in front of the lorry entrance he gave a quick glance in the yard, but all appeared to be empty. He hesitated for a moment and then made straight for the side door and stairs. His plan was to reconnoitre as swiftly as possible, and if, as was almost certain, he encountered someone, to say that he was interested in buying the property. As quietly as possible he went up the first flight to find himself opposite two closed doors. He knocked quietly on the first one and receiving no answer he noiselessly turned the handle. The door gave and he found himself inside quite a large room overlooking the river. A quick glance round assured him that there was nothing in the room except a pile of twenty or thirty suitcases. He listened by the door for a moment. All was quiet.

In two strides he was over to the suitcases. Quickly he pulled back the clasp and opened one. It was empty. He tried the next and the next, but they were the same. He turned away for a moment, bewildered. A pile of empty suitcases just didn't make sense. Then quickly he crossed the room and slipped out into the passage. Again he stood listening for a while outside the other door, but nothing could be heard. He knocked again gently and was about to open the door when:

'Come in!' he heard faintly from within. He entered. A man was sitting at a roll desk, his head bent over some papers. Two other men sat on chairs beside the window. Roger's pulses quickened as he sensed the lack of business atmosphere.

The man at the desk raised his head, and for a second his eyes opened wide with surprise at seeing a stranger. The next instant they had half closed again, as the man recovered his self-control.

'Good afternoon,' began Roger. 'Would you please tell me where I can make enquiries about this property? I wanted to know if it is likely to come into the market in the next year or two.'

The man at the desk passed a hand over his bald head and stared at Roger reflectively. He took a cigarette from a packet which lay on the desk and, striking a match, inhaled deeply.

'This property — is not — for sale,' he said heavily, with a faint foreign accent, and blew out the match.

Simple words, and a simple action, yet

— perhaps because the whole time his eyes did not leave Roger's face — Roger found an indescribable menace in them.

He determined to beat a swift retreat. 'I beg your pardon,' he apologised. 'In that case there is no use my continuing my enquiries,' and he turned to go.

'Wait a minute — please!' came the voice from the desk, and the two men at the window straightened themselves. 'I am always interested in gentlemen who wish to make — enquiries . . . What is it you wished to know?'

Roger turned back to him quite casually. 'Well, I'm afraid it's not much use if this property is not for sale, but I noticed that the four premises adjoining here are all for sale. As they are, of course, they're no use, but with this end they make quite a nice piece of property. That's what made me come up to make the enquiry.'

'I see.'

There was a definite lightening in the tension, and Roger hoped that his explanation had sounded plausible. He was just about to renew his farewells, with a hope that they would be accepted this time, when there was another knock. At a gesture from the man at the desk, one of the watchers at the window crossed over to open the door. There was an exchange of whispers with the newcomer, and then the latter came in. As he caught sight of Roger, he stopped short in surprise.

'What, you here!' he exclaimed blankly. It was the man who had been talking to Anne.

'You know him?' The question came like a pistol shot from the desk.

'Well — er — no, sir!' the man was confused at the result of his surprised remark. Then, 'He was in the café with a girl, sir! She's waiting there for him!' he proffered by way of explanation.

'So! . . . You always take a lady friend with you to make enquiries about property, and then leave her in a café, Mr. — ? You did not tell me your name!'

'Mr. Garrett!' supplemented Roger uneasily. Luck was certainly not travelling his way. 'That was my typist. I take her with me in case I have some reports for her to take down on the spot.'

'How very useful!' was the ironic answer. 'I am sorry, Mr. — Garrett — to have to ask these personal questions, but we have been troubled lately with some — unpleasant — characters in this district.' The tone was definitely mocking now.

'You will, I'm sure, not object if we ask your typist to come along to verify what you have said!'

Ferningham groaned inwardly. He could not take the risk of allowing Anne to come here, yet he did not see how he was going to prevent it.

But the other did not wait for an answer to his question.

'Williams,' he continued, to one of the men at the window. 'Just go along with Driscoll here. He will point out the girl to you. Tell her Mr. Garrett would like her to come with you. Mr. Garrett will wait here for you, I know.'

As he finished speaking, Ferningham realised that his story was entirely disbelieved. His only hope now was to bluff, and to bluff hard.

'One minute there, you need not take

that message, because I'm just going there myself!'

The three men converged on the door with ominous lack of words.

'Stop this tomfoolery, and stand aside there,' Ferningham rapped out as his way was barred.

'Sit down, Mr. Garrett!' There was a new tone in the man's voice. Roger half turned to find himself looking into the blue nose of an automatic.

'You have a novel way of inviting people to take a seat!' he remarked with a sudden calm.

'Quite a new one!' the other agreed. 'It's a device for dealing with burglars. I had a burglar once, you know. I was so sorry for him. But what could I do? He wouldn't stop, and I called out to him quite loudly!'

'So I've got to stay here until my typist comes, to repeat to you what I have already told you!' said Roger with a last attempt at bluff.

'I'm afraid so, but that won't be long. Williams has already gone.'

A glance out of the window confirmed

his statement. The two men were already turning the corner. Roger waited, helpless and sick at heart. He dared not do anything except acquiesce. For himself he cared not; had it been only a question of himself, he would already have made a dash for it, and trusted to luck; but with Anne within easy reach he dared not take the risk. Their one chance now remained in keeping cool.

He lit a cigarette and was gratified to note that his hands were perfectly steady. Wildly and unreasonably he hoped that Anne might have left the café.

'I told you that it would not be long.' The voice broke in on his thoughts. At the implication of the words, Roger looked again out of the window. Anne was already half-way to the door, the man Williams by her side.

The man at the desk lifted the receiver of the house telephone by his side.

'Grayson and Edwards, please . . . yes — yes . . . up here!' As he spoke into the receiver his eyes never left Roger's face. Footsteps sounded on the stairs. The door opened and two more men entered. Their leader waved them to one side, and they took up their positions against the further wall, without speaking, their eyes on Roger.

Once more footsteps sounded. It was Anne and Williams arriving. Roger's left hand slowly clenched and unclenched.

'Open the door!' said the man at the desk very softly.

Anne was the first to enter.

'Roger,' she began, and then, catching sight of the other four, she was silent.

'Miss Troy,' began Roger, hurriedly yet formally, 'I am sorry that you should be dragged here, but this gentleman does not believe that I am an agent for — '

'One moment,' broke in the leader. 'You will excuse me if I question your — er — friend. Miss Troy,' he continued smoothly, 'your employer's name, please?'

'Mr. — er — Garrett.'

'And his occupation?'

'Agent.'

'Mr. Garrett — however — has just used the word.'

'He is a property agent,' amended Anne briefly, but with inward qualms lest Roger should have changed their plan of campaign. As she answered, however, she could see that the answer was right. The man seemed definitely at a loss how to proceed. But only for a moment, then:

'And what property is he examining today, Miss Troy?'

She hesitated for a moment, then, with sudden inspiration:

'If Mr. Garrett does not feel inclined to discuss such details of his business with you, it is certainly not my business to do so,' she countered with warmth.

'But why not? Tell me, if you please, your relationship with Mr. Garrett.'

'Relationship,' she echoed hesitatingly.

Roger broke in, sensing the deep waters in which she was floundering.

'That is not meant as an insult, Miss Troy,' he jested. 'He means, are you actually my secretary.'

'Why — er — yes, of course I am,' Anne assented.

'Very clever, Mr. Garrett, but perhaps a little too clever. It is a funny thing,' the man at the desk continued, rising and coming in front of Roger: 'I never forget a face — and you remind me of someone — it worries me. And your business, too, Mr. Garrett. You have a secretary, a typist, and you take her with you and leave her to wait in uncomfortable cafés. And then she comes in and calls you 'Roger.' Comes in and calls you 'Roger,'' he repeated in a whisper. 'Roger, Roger ... So!' It was a shout rather than an exclamation as the little man whirled on Roger Ferningham. 'So!' he repeated, softly this time with a long-drawn-out breath. 'I remember now!'

His hand dropped into his pocket, as Roger stared at him, and emerged again, holding the automatic.

'You — are — not — dead — then, Mr. — FERNINGHAM!' His voice rose, so that the name was almost shouted.

Anne uttered a gasp and sprang to Roger's side.

But as quickly as the man had lost his self-control, equally as quickly he regained it.

'I am so sorry for startling you,' he apologised, 'but really, you know, for a moment you startled even me! ... Yes

. . . yes — now I know why I could find your face familiar . . .

'So you escaped, Mr. Ferningham?' he continued, lighting another cigarette. 'That was so very clever of you. I should have liked to hear all about it, but — you see — I have no time!' His voice was dropping almost to a whisper.

'You see, Mistaire Ferningham' — the foreign accent was more pronounced now — 'what that girl so tragically died for, and what you — alas — were meant to die for — is something which is to happen tonight. Yes — after tonight I shall have money, more money than you would ever know what to do with . . . But I know! . . . ' His voice was rising now. 'Tomorrow that money will be all over England, Mistaire Ferningham. And in a month's time there will be no England!

'What a pity that you will not be alive!' He spoke with genuine regret. 'You will miss the greatest revolution of all time! What Russia has seen will be nothing — nothing at all! And it will be through ME!'

Roger felt a cold shiver down his back.

Mad the other man might be; undoubtedly was, in fact! But that he had power to wreak his madness, Ferningham did not doubt. Putting aside, however, their plight, it was still vital to know as much of the gang's plans as possible, and now was the moment, if any, to draw the leader into unwary confidences.

He therefore assumed an incredulous yet mocking air at the sound of the other's boast.

'If you imagine that ten thousand, or even a hundred thousand, pounds are going to turn England upside down, I'm afraid you're in for a disappointment, little man,' he countered with a smile.

'But not two million pounds,' the other replied softly, ignoring the jibe at his stature.

Ferningham whistled with amazement. 'Two million!' he repeated in a dazed voice. 'But you'd have to own a bank to get that in cash today!'

'Exactly . . . Mistaire Ferningham . . . we shall own a bank . . . for two hours!' The other chuckled as he caught sight of Roger's face.

'It is so easy . . . when I am in charge! Do you know what is below us, and behind us? The river . . . Mistaire Ferningham! And at our landing stage is a motor launch, which will hold a hundred suit cases. The suit cases are there — oh, yes, but they are empty now. Tomorrow they will have twenty thousand pounds in each of them, and where do you think they will go? They will go up the river, not far, to a garage. It is my garage. In that garage are fifty cars. Two suit cases for each, and in half an hour those cars will be on the roads all over England. And because tomorrow I shall own a bank for two hours. In a month, Mr. Ferningham, I shall own England!'

Ferningham could only shake his head in obstinate refusal to believe.

'You do not think so?' the other caught him up swiftly. 'You think this England of yours is so safe? That its men will work and work, watching others play! How many years is it since your manor lords possessed every peasant's body on their lands? And today, your capitalist, he holds their very souls! There is a voice, Mistaire

Ferningham, which cries out today, from every slum, from every factory in this country! And because you cannot hear it, you think it is not there! . . . But I hear it . . . and tomorrow the whole world will hear it!

'And so, Mistaire Ferningham, I will keep you alive for just a little time . . . until tomorrow, shall we say? And you shall be allowed to see the beginning!'

He finished, exhausted by his speech, and wiped his forehead.

'Very convincing,' said Roger calmly, with an effort. 'But I still don't see why I should die because you think you are collecting two million pounds. Or, for that matter, why you should be so concerned for our slums and our factories.'

'Perhaps,' the other replied, 'it is because I knew a man who came to England not many years ago. He came to England because they told him it was free, because they told him men were equal. In the country where he lived they used once only to talk of America.

'Yes, Mr. Ferningham, when I was

fourteen, when I was watching my father and mother die, I saved my money, kopek by kopek, because they told me of America. Two hundred kopeks was what my sister needed to live. I had not got two hundred kopeks, so she disappeared. I knew then that I should never disappear.

'It takes a long time to save money in the country where I was born, and so, one day, they told me of a place called London, which would not need so many kopeks to arrive at. And so I came here.

'Would you like to know what happened? I arrived at a station. I did not know your language, I did not know your people. But they told me you were free in England. And what did they do to me? They put me in gaol, Mr. Ferningham, because I sat on my bag in the doorway of a street, because I didn't know where to go. When I came out they put me in gaol again. I do not remember why it was.

'But this was my land of the free. I learnt to make button-holes when I came out again. Have you ever tried to earn your bread by sewing button-holes, Mr. Ferningham? In a little room with eighty others, with just the gas-light to warm you and bread to fill your stomach? And so then I swore that one day we *should* be free in England; but first, to be free we must have money.

'It did not take long. There have been some robberies; you may have read of them in your morning paper. There have been murders; I regret them. And then I found a way to get the money which your rich put into the banks instead of sharing with their workers.

'There was, as you will remember, Mr. Ferningham, a girl — Miss Webb. She worked for me, at first without any suspicions. But she also fell in love with my man Jake. He is not a clever man, this Jake. He is strong and he is obedient, but he talked to this girl. When all this is over, Mr. Jake will have earned a — holiday. Just now he is too useful. But I have not forgotten.

'There was too much at stake for this girl to go on living. But if she died — your police are so curious; they do not mind anyone starving; they do not mind anyone dying from starving; but they must not die too suddenly. And so I had to arrange that when she died there should be someone there to take the blame. I did not know you, and, believe me, I was very sorry for you. But since she was coming to you, it was best that you should be blamed by the police. In that way they would not worry about where she worked, and in that way I could finish my task in peace.

'And so, until tomorrow, you will wait upstairs, Mr. Ferningham — you and your — typist. A little discomfort, I'm afraid; but there' — with a wave of the hand — 'it is better to be tied up than — what is it you say? — screwed down.

'See these two safely upstairs,' he ordered. Then, turning again to Ferningham, 'Please do not try to be rash,' he warned him. He was about to say more when the telephone rang. Crossing to the table, he lifted the receiver. 'Five Three Seven Five,' he called. Then, over his shoulder. 'Take them away,' he ordered.

11

The Central Bank, Lombard Street, is one of the world's great institutions. Its cashiers receive and dispense money in every great city, its circular cheques are known in every big hotel throughout the Continent. The millions which it lends to governments are drawn as the sands of the sea from Land's End to John o'Groats, Calcutta to the Cape.

An Indian rajah was a client — so, as it happened, was Mrs. Benson.

Now a bank does not only handle money. Stocks and shares, insurance policies, deeds, wills and legacies; passports and safe custodies, all these are within their legal activities. In fact, the most important thing in the work of the clerks is something else than money, for to thousands of bank clerks money means mere rows of figures; credit figures and debit figures which it is their lifelong work to balance.

But if not money, then what? The answer is PAPER! Shoals upon shoals of paper forms, debit slips and credit slips, cheque forms and receipt forms. Tons upon tons of paper. So one does not necessarily need to deal in finance to be a banker. Mr. Howard was a case in point. Forty years before these events, young Howard had joined the bank with the ambition of being a world controller of finance. Today, Mr. Howard was the bank controller of paper. He was the manager of the Stationery Department; but this did not stop his wife from alluding to him on any and every occasion as 'my husband the financier.'

Mr. Howard did not confine his activities solely to buying paper; he had to sell it as well. Banks accumulate tons of waste paper. Some of this paper is very confidential. It has to be sold, of course, because no bank can afford to lose the chance of making any money. It would not be fair to their principles to give anything away. In the case of the Central Bank, it had very strong ideas of preserving every atom of secrecy about their customers. The waste paper of hundreds of branches was collected and sent to London for sale under contract to a waste paper company. Now, Mr. Howard was a keen business man; so, when six months before, he had received a very favourable tender from a new waste paper company, he had accepted it. This company was brought to his notice by his personal secretary.

It takes time to put a tender through, but now the day had arrived, and down below in the Bank's strong-rooms were dozens and dozens of sacks of waste paper waiting to be collected the following morning.

This, then, was the position at four o'clock on this momentous afternoon when Mr. Howard rang his buzzer for his secretary. This was Miss Wilkinson. As she came in, notebook in hand, she looked the epitome of banking efficiency. Tall, neatly-dressed, with a face entirely devoid of expression, pince-nez balanced accurately on her nose, she was a tribute to the acumen of the Central Bank in their selection of staff. Mr. Howard could hardly refrain from sighing with satisfaction as he looked at that competent face.

'No more letters, Miss Wilkinson?'

'No, Mr. Howard.'

'Good. You've confirmed that the waste paper is to be collected at eight o'clock tomorrow morning?'

'Yes, sir. The commissionaire is having the sacks put ready in the passage, and will be here early tomorrow to superintend the loading.'

'Very well, Miss Wilkinson. I'll be leaving now. Good-day.'

'Good-day, sir,' his secretary answered dutifully.

The door closed behind him, and for a long moment she sat there gazing before her. Then, observing that it was a quarter past four, she reached for the 'phone. With unerring fingers she dialled the Exchange, and then 5 — 3 — 7 — 5. There was half-a-minute's pause, then —

'5 — 3 — 7 — 5' sounded on the 'phone.

'I shall be waiting outside from half-past four onwards . . . yes . . . Both will be leaving before five.' With which cryptic message she hung up the receiver.

She crossed the room and entered the inner office where she kept her coat and hat. Unhurriedly she put them on, picked up her handbag, and made her way to the corridor. She stopped at the sixth door, labelled 'General Manager, Enquiries,' and opened it. The girl inside smiled up at her. 'Hallo, Miss Wilkinson.'

'Hallo, Miss Pym! Day's work over?'

'Yes, just finishing. The old man's just clearing off now.'

'He is, is he? That's a nuisance. Miss Pym, do me a favour, will you? Hold on to him for about a quarter of an hour. I don't want him to bump into the stationery manager on the way out, because, if he does, I shall have another couple of letters to write.'

'Blast you!' said Miss Pym genially. 'Right ho! I'll work up a query or two for him to gnash his teeth on!'

'Thanks, Pym,' said the other quietly, and closed the door without more ado.

At the end of the corridor she stopped again, this time outside an office marked 'Chief Accountant.'

Again she opened the door and

accosted the typist at work inside.

''Evening, Grace! Nearly finished?'

'Oh, hallo, Miss Wilkinson. Yes, the C.A. will be off in another half an hour, thank the Lord!'

Miss Wilkinson nodded in response, and wishing the girl good-bye, she passed into the lift. Downstairs in the main hall the clerks were working feverishly to finish the day's balance.

She walked down the main aisle towards the central doors, and bidding the commissionaire good-night, she stepped out on to the steps.

She stood there for a full two minutes, when suddenly from the neighbouring clocks the half hour began to strike. At the same moment her gaze focussed itself on the two cars already drawing up not twenty feet away, one a private car, the other a new taxi.

She crossed the road and paused by the first one. There were three men inside.

'The General Manager will be out in about five minutes,' she said unemotionally. 'You know him by sight?' The driver nodded.

'You will see the car brought round by a garage man. The manager drives it himself. Don't attempt anything until you get to his place. He always gets out to undo the gates.' The driver nodded again without speaking.

She turned to the taxi. 'Cruise round for another quarter of an hour, then pull up at the Bank steps. Just say to the commissionaire, 'Mr. Downing's taxi.' He'll think that the chief accountant has ordered it, so when the accountant comes out he'll bring him to you. The accountant always takes a taxi, so he'll think that you are just a cruising taxi that the commissionaire has got for him. Once he's in, take him fifty yards up the road, where you, Thomas,' turning to the man inside, 'will be waiting for him. Then you get into the cab with him; just show him a gun, you won't have to do anything more. Then from there drive to the garage, he'll be collected from there.'

'That'll be all right,' said the man at the wheel.

'It's got to be!' she countered. 'You'd better cruise with me inside so that no one else will want you.' With that she opened the door or the cab and got in. With a smooth snick of the gears, the taxi moved off.

The other car had not long to wait. Within a quarter of an hour there drew up at the Bank steps a shining saloon, and a man in overalls, obviously a garage hand, descended.

Half a minute later an elderly man descended the steps, spoke to the garage hand for a moment, then entered the car and drove off. Thirty yards behind him followed the second car. Inside, the three men were arguing.

'Hope to God,' grumbled the first, 'that he doesn't drive too fast, or we'll be getting to Gerrard's Cross in daylight.'

'Sure we'll get there in daylight,' broke in the second, 'and what the hell! You'll be able to see what you're killing. His house is half a mile from the next one, isn't it? We've been four times along this road, and never met a soul yet, have we?'

'Yes, but I've got to do ten miles after that, with a body in the back, and a car belonging to the body.'

'Oh, can it!' said the other disgustedly, and the party relapsed into silence.

But as though in obedience to their wishes, the car in front proceeded at a very gentle pace, and dusk had already fallen when they reached the outskirts of Gerrard's Cross.

'Step on it now, Alf!' muttered the man beside the driver. 'We've got to be well before him.'

As the accelerator button went down, the car leapt forward and passed the first as they entered the town. As they reached the highway they turned right, and made for the outskirts. The manager in his saloon was already sixty yards behind.

'Left it a bit late,' muttered the driver. 'We've only another mile and a half.'

'Time enough,' grunted the man beside him. They were passing large houses now, each in an acre or more of its own garden, and in another minute the car came to a sudden stop. Obviously acting on a rehearsed scheme, the two passengers leapt out and made for the drive of the last house they had just passed.

Hurriedly one of them ducked, slipped

through the gate to the drive and ran up a few yards. 'All clear,' he called softly. Then came the sound of the other car approaching.

The man who was left had paused on the path by the gate, and was feeling in his pockets.

The car drew up with a scrunch of tyres on the gravel, and the manager opened the car door and prepared to descend.

As he did so, the man on the path moved his hands. Then came a sharp click! click! and the manager sank back with a groaning gasp. His leg, hanging out over the running-board, twitched violently and was still.

'O.K.!' said the man as he removed the silencer from his gun. The other joined him. Together they opened the rear door of the saloon, and with a heave they lifted the body out of the driving seat and into the rear. The gunman carefully propped him up in the corner, so that the head rested back against the cushions.

'Nice work, Alf!' said the other cheerfully.

'Betcherlife!' replied Alf warmly. He reached

in his pocket for a cigarette, found one, and poised it between the dead man's lips. 'Can't waste a cigar on you!' he jested. Then: 'Come in, into the front.'

They got into the front together, and with a smooth acceleration they moved off.

In front the driver of the other car waved them on and followed in their trail.

'Did you frisk him on the way, Alf, for the keys?' enquired the passenger.

'No. Wait until we get to the quarry,' said the other.

They were heading now in the direction of Slough, and short as had been the time taken, it was now dark.

Alf drove carefully, watching the right-hand side of the road. At length he grunted with satisfaction and swung right down a narrow country lane, switching off his headlights as he straightened up after the turn. Twenty yards behind, the second car followed suit. They were travelling now at barely twelve miles an hour, their sidelights only faintly illuminating the ditches and hedgerows which pressed in on them so closely.

'First gate,' muttered Alf, as they

passed a battered gateway. ''Bout another hundred yards.' He eased the car down to walking pace, switching off the sidelights as he did so. The second gate loomed up, and Alf drew back the hand brake. For half a minute they sat there, listening intently, but nothing moved.

'Seems all clear,' said Alf in a low voice. 'Better have a scout round, though.' The two descended from the car.

'Where's the other car?'

'Waiting at the first gate! Easier to turn there, and we don't want too many tracks down here! Be able to warn us, too, if anyone comes down the road!'

'Ground's dry enough round the gate! Shouldn't show the tyres.'

'No, thank the Lord! Come on, let's get the gate open!'

Swiftly they opened the gate, turned back to the car, and pushed it through. Inside the field was a cart track leading fairly sharply down for a hundred yards into a disused pit. Alf climbed into the driver's seat. 'Give me a push and I'll be able to take her down on the brake,' he muttered.

The other obeyed, and as the car gently gathered way he leapt on to the running-board. At the bottom Alf headed her deliberately for a clump of bushes. There was a crunch as the foliage gave way in front, then the car came to rest. The two descended, and turned to a pile of corrugated iron sheets about half a dozen yards away. Carefully, yet to give the impression of carelessness, they stacked three sheets round the back of the car, completely hiding it from the sight of anyone who might be passing along the road above next morning.

Then, slipping through the bushes to the driving seat, Alf wriggled over to the back seat. Rapidly he turned out the pockets of the dead man, until a bunch of keys came to light. He gave another grunt of satisfaction as he pocketed them. Then methodically he continued to transfer everything else he found to his own pockets. The search completed, he joined his companion.

'O.K.?' asked the latter. Alf nodded and looked at his watch, with its luminous dial.

'Ten minutes behind time. We shall have to move!' he commented and led the way up the steep track. At the top they paused to secure the gate, then, whistling a popular song, they strolled back along the road. Seventy yards away the refrain was echoed from the waiting car, a signal for 'All Clear.'

Within a few seconds they came abreast the other driver.

'Turned the car round, then?' grunted Alf with satisfaction.

'Everything jake?'

'Sure! And the old boy carried some good cigars. Here we are, one apiece, and let's get moving!'

'Which way? Through Slough?'

'Yes, turn her off at Chiswick! Stop at Slough first, though, to 'phone the O.K. through. We've got an hour and a half, so we've got to move!'

'Well, if they got the accountant so easily . . . '

'Sure they've got him! Davies and Jake know their work!' The car sped swiftly through the night.

As it happened, Davies and Jake knew

their work only too well.

At ten minutes to five the taxi had drawn up, and Davies, the driver, had told the commissionaire that he was ordered for the chief accountant. The latter came down the Bank steps a minute later, and at the commissionaire's 'Your taxi, sir,' had got in unsuspectingly.

He did not even look up for a moment when the taxi stopped in Upper Thames Street. When he did, it was to find Jake opening the door with one hand and covering him with a gun with the other.

'Move over, Buddy!' grunted Jake as he stepped in. 'And don't yell! You'll wake the baby!'

The accountant was not of the stuff that heroes are made. He shrank into the further corner, and thereafter uttered not a word. Swiftly the taxi made its way towards Rotherhithe and the garage. Instead of drawing up outside the latter, however, the taxi continued right in. As it came to a standstill a man in overalls stepped forward, eyebrows raised in silent enquiry, to the driver. Davies nodded back towards the inside of the cab. The man in overalls opened the door.

''Lo, Jake,' he greeted the gunman. Then:

'Welcome 'ome, little stranger!' The accountant remained speechless, huddled in the cab.

'I said 'Welcome 'ome,'' repeated the man in overalls, 'which means 'op out, and do it quickly.'

The accountant made haste to obey.

'Where! . . . Where! . . . Where! . . . ' he stammered unhappily.

'Save it, stranger!' menaced Jake, his gun still in his hand. Then, turning to the man in overalls: 'Where's the car?'

The other nodded to a saloon standing near-by.

'Tell Davies to take it steady. She's got a pretty fierce clutch. I'll give them a ring to say that you're on your way.'

'Right! Come on, Mister Banker, we're off again,' jested Jake. 'And keep your claptrap shut!' he added fiercely but unnecessarily.

The unfortunate chief accountant climbed miserably into the rear of the saloon. For over thirty years he had led a peaceful life in the service of the Bank. By assiduous toil he had risen from a humble junior to the control of several hundred clerks. Now, at fifty-five, he was meeting for the first time a type of man outside his accustomed ken. It was small blame to him that he failed so completely to cope with them. A warning anent the clutch to Davies, and they were off.

In five minutes they were at the factory. Carefully Jake shepherded his prisoner upstairs, while Davies took the car back. In the office they were awaiting his arrival.

'Now you can talk, and talk plenty!' remarked Jake, as he pushed the other into the room.

The man at the desk looked up at their entry.

'You are Mr. Aldington, Chief Accountant of the London and Central Bank?'

'I am; but what . . . ?'

'Be quiet, Mr. Aldington, for a moment. You are one of the holders of the Bank's strong-room keys?'

'I am.'

'Thank you. The other is the General

Manager! Tonight, Mr. Aldington, you will open the strong-rooms in the company of my men!'

'That is impossible . . . I . . . '

'It is not impossible. It happens that you are going to do it.'

The accountant looked desperately at the men who stood round him.

'You can't force me. You can do what you like, but I . . . '

'Have you seen the evening paper, Mr. Aldington? You haven't?' The man behind the desk idly picked up a paper lying beside him, and tossed it lightly across. His eyes were fixed on the accountant's face. With trembling fingers the latter picked it up and, following the other's pointing finger, read the Stop Press: 'Two bodies found in Pimlico house,' he read.

'Two men I used to know,' murmured the man at the desk. 'They will be the headlines tomorrow morning . . . Have you been in the headlines, Mr. Aldington?'

The accountant winced at the other's measured words. His face went grey.

'But how do I know that you won't kill me afterwards, and — in any case I

218

haven't got the General Manager's set.' But even as he blurted out his objections, he knew that the question of the keys was already settled.

'You don't know, Mistaire Aldington; you can only hope! . . . And do not worry about the other keys. I will not forget them!'

'But I beg of you, sir . . . if I do this . . . if . . . it will be ruin . . . my wife . . . two children . . . '

'Yes, yes! You will stay here until ten o'clock tonight, when you will accompany my men to the Bank. But in the meantime I had not forgotten your wife or your two dear little children either. So now, Mr. Aldington, you will telephone your wife and your two little children, and you will tell them how sorry you are that urgent banking business will keep you in Town for tonight. You may comfort them, however, by explaining that this business will make a great change in your future! . . . Kindly repeat to me what you are going to say!'

Aldington wiped his brow with an unsteady hand.

'I shall be staying in Town tonight, darling,' he spoke tremblingly, mechanically, yet such was the tenseness in the room that not a person smiled as the term of affection left his lips, incongruous though it sounded in such an assembly.

'Important banking business has just turned up which I must not miss . . . It will mean a big change in my future, though; . . . a . . . big . . . change.' His voice tailed off as he uttered the last ironic words.

'That will do quite well,' agreed his captor, 'but do not forget to impress on her not to worry. No, no, here is the telephone; do not make any stupid mistake!'

With his left hand he indicated the telephone, his right hand held a gun.

The accountant stood still a moment, as if mentally bracing himself. Then, with a noticeable effort at steadiness, he picked up the receiver and called a number. There was silence in the room while he was being connected, then he began to speak:

'Is that you, dear? . . . Jim speaking! I shan't be home tonight; there's some very important banking business suddenly turned up which I must not miss . . . Yes, yes; oh, quite all right, my dear, don't worry . . . Yes, as a matter of fact, it should make a great difference to me . . . Yes . . . very well. Good-bye, my dear, my love to the children, and yourself . . . Good-bye.' His voice throughout was surprisingly steady.

'And what did your wife say?'

'She said it would be all right!'

'I'm sure we all hope so!' murmured the man at the desk. At that moment the telephone rang back. The leader flashed his gun in sudden suspicion at the accountant, then as suddenly he relaxed.

'But, of course — she does not know your number,' he explained. He did not put his gun away, however, but drew the receiver over with his other hand.

'Hello,' he said, and listened for a minute; then, 'Good, very good! Come straight on here! . . . Good-bye!'

He turned to the accountant with a smile.

'Just a message to say that you will have the General Manager's keys to help you tonight.'

The accountant made no reply, and the other man turned to the telephone book. He found the number he wanted and turned to the telephone again. 'Mr. Arbuthnot asked me to leave a message for Mrs. Arbuthnot. He is detained in Town tonight with an important business meeting, and will not be home tonight . . . Thank you . . . Good-bye!'

At the sound of the name, the accountant had straightened himself. As though answering a question, the other remarked in an apologetic tone:

'Yes, I had to telephone on behalf of the General Manager. He is unable to do so himself, poor man!'

12

There was a little clock on the mantelpiece of the room in which Mr. Aldington the accountant sat with his two gaolers. Mechanically, he watched its hands creep round from seven to eight, from eight to nine. His two children would be in bed by now, fast asleep. His wife, he knew, would be sitting up late to finish his pullover. It was his birthday in three days' time, and she still had half the back and one sleeve to finish.

He wondered vaguely if he would ever use it. He did not feel afraid any longer, only apathetic. Davies and Jake, the two warders, had offered to cut him in on a game of poker, but he had refused, because he did not know how to play. It was not a game which bank clerks were encouraged to learn. But he almost wished that he had learnt it; it would have been something to stop him from thinking.

At ten o'clock they offered him a bottle of beer, and he accepted it gratefully. It was a little difficult to drink without the use of a glass, and at first he had a fit of coughing. But he managed to finish the bottle.

At ten minutes to eleven the door opened and the little man, who seemed to be the leader, came in.

'Time to start work, Mr. Accountant. You are accustomed to work late in banks, are you not? The balance must be arranged twice a year. This is just another balance, Mr. Aldington, which I shall be settling tonight.'

He turned as he spoke to the man called Jake. 'You know what to do. Here are the other keys. You will give them to Mr. Aldington when you are in the Bank.'

He looked at his watch. 'You will be back at midnight,' he said, and left the room. Davies pushed back his chair, snatched the money from the table and got up. With a movement of his head towards the door he signalled to Aldington. The three of them went down the stairs.

To the left in the garage a car was already ticking over. There was another man in the back seat. The three of them climbed in.

'Don't attract attention, little playmate, or I'll smack a chunk of lead in your skull.' Jake had warned him as the car started off.

Swiftly they sped through the nearly deserted streets, up past the Monument and across into Poultry. As they slowed up, Jake leaned forward to compare his watch with the clock on the dashboard.

The car drew up at a side entrance of the Central Bank. Jake looked up and down the street. The pavement was deserted. There was not a policeman in sight.

'Make it half an hour exactly by your clock, Davies.' Jake was already climbing out. 'Come on, Mister Accountant, and look cheerful. Just aim to walk as though you liked it!'

'Half an hour prompt,' replied Davies, and threw in his clutch.

Casually the other three strolled over to the side door. Jake gently rang the door bell. It opened immediately and they stepped in.

'Fasten up!' ordered Jake unnecessarily, for the watchman was already shooting home the bolts. 'How's the other man?'

'Tied up below; bumped him a bit too hard, I think; but I had to make sure.'

Aldington's heart sank as he recognised the watchman. He had been employed by the Bank for several years now, so that his defection argued that the gang was considerably better organised than he had imagined.

As to their exact plans he was still in ignorance, but their confidence of success filled him with terror. Trembling, he awaited the orders which he dared not disobey.

'O.K.,' continued Jake with complete lack of emotion. 'You've moved the sacks of paper back downstairs? Good. Let's go!' A prod informed Aldington that he was included in the invitation. In single file they descended a flight of stairs, which led — as the luckless accountant knew only too well — to the underground vaults. The night watchman, who answered to the name of Graham, led the way. Aldington came next, and Jake followed with the other member of the car load.

They were well below street level now, and the air was definitely cooler. Down one long corridor they went, turned right, and then right again.

The strong-rooms of the Bank, in fact, formed an island in the middle of the corridors, so that its four walls were entirely detached from any party wall. As they came to the front of the strong-room, the accountant understood the reference to the sacks of paper. Stacked in rows were the eighty sacks of waste paper, which the Bank, as he knew, were dispatching first thing in the morning. He wondered why they had been moved downstairs, but was not long in doubt.

Jake had stopped and was examining the seven-foot square steel door of the vault with undisguised admiration.

'Swell job!' he muttered; then, 'Well, buddy,' he challenged the accountant, 'fetch out your bunches of can-openers and get busy. We've got twenty-five minutes to do our stuff, and if it takes us twenty-six — well, it'll be just too bad for you!'

'You mean open the doors?' stammered Aldington.

'Sure! You've got both sets of keys. Well, use 'em!'

The accountant obeyed. There were two clicks, and he turned to the bolt lever and threw it back. Then he gave a heave on the handle, and the massive door, over a foot thick, swung back on its hinges. There was a grill door beyond, again guarded by two locks which opened inwards.

'And now, Happy, let's have all the cash boxes open, them that holds the paper money!' They were standing in the strongroom now, surrounded by stacks of boxes, and by no less than four safes.

In silence the accountant crossed over to the nearest safe, eight feet high. He selected a key from each bunch and stooped to the locks. There were clicks as the tumblers dropped, then he threw back the bolt and straightened himself. 'New Treasury notes, pound and ten shillings,' he announced in a dull voice, and without waiting for any answer he moved on to the next.

'Bank notes,' he called out in the same mechanical voice, and crossed over to the left-hand wall. Here he proceeded to open box after box, saying as he did so, 'Used notes!'

After the twelfth box, he faced the others. 'Those are all the notes, you can check them by the cash summary reserve books upstairs,' he said wearily. 'If you want the gold, it is in the third safe,' he finished.

'Guess we can only handle the notes,' murmured Jake regretfully. 'Now, boys, we've got twenty minutes. Get the cash outside, empty the sacks in the strong-room, and fill them up with the notes. Put some waste paper in the top of each sack.

Feverishly, but methodically, they set to work, the accountant forced to help the rest. Ten minutes passed, and they were only a third done.

'Put the pressure on, boys,' came the warning from Jake, and they redoubled their efforts. Nineteen minutes, and they were on their last sack.

'Fine,' said Jake. 'We've got six minutes. Heave those boxes in! You've got the bank note register books, Mister Accountant? . . . thanks!' As Aldington pointed to three half-bound volumes which he had already taken out of the strongroom under instructions. He handed them to the night watchman.

'Bung 'em in the furnace, Graham. We don't want people checking up on the numbers.'

'What about the cashier's books upstairs?'

'Burn those too. They won't be asking for them until nine o'clock, and we'll be clear by then . . . Now, Mister Accountant, let's look at the strong-room keys!' Aldington handed over the two bunches, indicating the requisite keys.

'Thanks a lot,' said the other, 'and now, supposing you just step back in that strong-room!'

The accountant stared at him in sudden terror, his face twitching.

'In there . . . in . . . you're not going to leave me there?'

'Get in!'

'But — but . . . ' A brutal shove and the

accountant sprawled back amongst the mountain of waste paper heaped up on the strong-room floor. He started to rise, but floundered in the pile. His eyes distended with fear; he opened his mouth to call out, but even as he did so, there was a muffled plop, plop, plop, as Jake poured bullet after bullet into him.

'So yeller it was a real pleasure,' was Jake's epitaph as he shut the grill door. He gave a quick glance round as he shut the outer door of the strong-room and applied the keys.

'Get rid of any bits of paper, and get the sacks up again. You know what to tell the commissionaire when he comes? The lorry will be here at eight o'clock. Everything O.K.?'

'I'll be all right.'

'Sure you will. C'mon, let's go!'

13

'Past eleven, Ma; I don't like it, and that's a fact!' Biggs was seated opposite Mrs. Benson in her parlour, and as he spoke he anxiously gazed at the old-fashioned clock on the mantelshelf.

'No sign of Miss Eversleigh, either! What are we going to do?'

'Well, the Major's instructions were not to move until tomorrow morning . . .'

'And then fetch the police,' Mrs. Benson broke in. 'Which is just what we are not going to do. I know, I know . . .' as Biggs opened his mouth in ineffectual argument. 'It may have been what he said, but we can do better than that.'

'You mean, we are going to try to pull it off ourselves. But how do you think we are going to set about it?'

'Never mind about that now! What you're going to have is a few hours' sleep. We can't do anything until tomorrow morning, and if you don't tuck yourself

232

up now I shall be having a hospital case on my hands. And though I didn't mind being a nurse on the stage, seeing it was my job, it is quite enough to cook your meals, without having to bath you.'

'And what are *you* going to do, old gal?'

'Think!' replied Mrs. Benson heavily. 'One of us has got to!'

And in point of fact, it was three hours later when she retired. When she did, it was merely to throw herself down on her bed without even troubling to remove her shoes.

Promptly at six o'clock she woke up, and for the next quarter of an hour busied herself in the kitchen and in the yard. Which done, she called Biggs.

'Breakfast in ten minutes, and look sharp. No . . . ' as Biggs started to question her. 'I'll tell you about it at breakfast. It is the best thing I can think of, and I don't want you to argue about it.' She avoided further discussion by returning to the kitchen, where she soon had the breakfast under way.

'Now,' she began, as she faced Biggs

across the table, 'this is what we are going to do! You know that huge pram that was left here last year? Well, I filled it up with newspapers and the like. We are going to take a taxi with the pram — that is, if we can find a taxi big enough to take it — and we are going down to the waste paper factory. We'll be pretending to sell the paper, and while we are there we'll see if we can find out anything funny going on. It is no use saying what we are going to do exactly until we get there. But at any rate this seems the best way of getting in. What's more, if they try any hanky-panky with me they will soon learn who I am.'

'And are we going to call in the police, Ma?'

'Maybe, and maybe not. It all depends on what happens there, but we'll have a good shot at doing without 'em. Now, if you have finished your meal, you can give me a hand with the pram.'

Biggs wiped his mouth and pushed back his chair.

'Hadn't I better get a taxi, Ma? We don't want to be standing in the street with a loaded pram for a quarter of an hour. Give the neighbours something more to talk about.'

'Which, seeing that they haven't had anything yet to talk about,' broke in Mrs. Benson belligerently, 'will be a change for them. Still, perhaps you are right,' she finished grudgingly. Biggs hurried to the door before she should change her mind. He was in luck's way, for a taxi was prowling not fifty yards away. Biggs whistled him over.

'Can you manage a large-sized pram, mate?' he asked the driver.

'Manage anything this time of morning,' replied the other cheerfully. 'In that case, 'ang on.' And Biggs disappeared to summon Mrs. Benson.

It was fully ten minutes before they had lodged the pram precariously on the roof of the taxi, and roped it down. It had been quite impossible to get it inside.

'Must have been intended for the 'Birth of a Nation,'' chuckled Biggs. Mrs. Benson laughed in reply, although the joke was as old as the hills. Then, giving the taxi-driver his instructions, they climbed into the cab.

'Well,' said Biggs a minute later, as he laid a hand affectionately on the landlady's knee, 'we are off now, and Gawd help us!'

The journey was an uneventful one, and there was comparative silence broken only by a jocular remark of Biggs anent his landlady's clothes. For Mrs. Benson, with all the thoroughness of an ex-actress, had seen fit to dress herself for the part. An ancient hat perched ominously over her left eyebrow. A tattered raincoat gaped in front to reveal an apron made of coarse sacking. In answer to his repeated questions as to the origin of the 'antiques,' she answered stiffly, 'Never you mind.' Mrs. Benson was on her dignity. Forty minutes later the taxi drew up a bare two hundred yards from the cul-de-sac where the waste paper factory had its entrance, and with considerable effort they got the pram down to the ground. Biggs winced at sight of the taximeter clock, but with a royal unconcern Mrs. Benson added two shillings by way of tips.

Together they watched the taxi depart, and for the first time the magnitude of their task was borne upon them. They made an odd couple as they stood there with the pram between them, but there was nothing of humour in their faces.

'Now then,' began Mrs. Benson at last, squaring her shoulders. 'Don't forget, Biggs, you are my husband, so I shall push the pram. When we get there, leave me to do the talking, and while I'm doing it, you see if you can wander round, casual-like, and find out what you can . . . Now, then, are you ready?'

'Ready it is,' said Biggs, with forced cheerfulness.

As they rounded the corner a near-by clock struck eight. The factory stood at the further end of the cul-de-sac, and as they approached it they could see that its main doors stood open.

'That's an entrance at the side, isn't it, Ma?' Biggs explained in a low voice. 'Looks as though it leads to the rooms above the factory. If I can get half a chance, I shall slip up there.'

'Well, mind you're careful!' Unafraid as

237

Mrs. Benson was where she herself was concerned, yet she could not view any independent action of Biggs without concern.

'That's all right, Ma. You just keep 'em talking, and if I get a chance to slip away, tell 'em I've gone off for a drink.'

As they wheeled the massive pram into the entrance, there was only one man on duty there. He did not seem pleased to see them; in fact, quite the reverse.

'What d'you want?' he demanded.

'Ah, wait till you see what I've brought yer,' said Mrs. Benson in a wheedling voice. With the gesture of a triumphant conjurer, she stripped the sacking from the top of the pram to reveal a heterogeneous mass of assorted waste paper.

'You'll be giving me a good price for this, I expect.' With which optimistic statement she gave a leer which embraced both Biggs and the surly workman.

'If that's all you've got, you can sling your hook as quick as you like,' he countered, viewing the pram with disgust.

'Sling me hook, eh? What are you

supposed to be, anyway? A waste paper factory, aren't yer? And what's this but waste paper, I should like to know! Been a' saving this 'ere paper for months I 'ave, and if you can't buy it, I shall soon know the reason why!'

The workman was obviously stunned at her volubility, and with an 'All right, all right, Ma, you just wait 'ere a minute,' he disappeared through a door at the rear.

'Now's me chance, old gal,' breathed Biggs.

'Good luck, then, and look after yourself.'

Biggs slipped away, leaving Mrs. Benson in sole charge of the pram.

Meanwhile, the workman had hurried up to the office on the first floor, where Ferningham had been trapped the evening before. The leader was still seated behind the desk as though he had not moved throughout the whole night. An ash-tray beside him overflowed with cigarette ends, and he was in the act of lighting another one as the man entered.

'Any news of the lorry?'

'No, sir, not yet. They'll be just about

loading it now. We should see them in about ten minutes.'

'What's the matter, then?'

'It is a woman downstairs, sir, wants to sell some paper. Seems as though she will be a bit difficult to send away.'

'Well, buy it, you damn fool! You don't want her around here when the lorry arrives. Are the suit cases all ready? And have you tested the engine of the launch?'

'Yes, sir, everything is ready. It shouldn't take more than ten minutes, once the lorry is back.'

'Good; then get rid of that damn woman. Pay her what you like so long as she is happy!' The man withdrew downstairs, missing Biggs by a fraction of a second. The latter, indeed, had paused outside the door only a few moments before, but upon hearing voices had continued up the stairs.

At the top landing he paused for a moment, steeling his nerves against the unknown. Then with a deep breath he tried the handle of the door. It opened. Slowly, very slowly, he opened it. There came no sound from within. Six inches, nine inches, a foot, and there was room for his head. Still no sound! Holding his breath, he peered into the room; the next moment he was inside! At the far end of the room, lying back upon the bed, were Angela and Ferningham, bound and gagged. Of their gaoler there was no sign. With three strides Biggs was across the room, fumbling in his pocket as he went. With a sigh of relief he produced an enormous clasp-knife.

'Found it first time,' he muttered gleefully. 'Now we won't be long, sir.' With surprising dexterity he had them free in under a minute.

'How in the Lord did you get here, Biggs?'

'The old lady is below, sir, selling them some paper. I slipped up when they wasn't listening. We haven't got long, sir. What shall we do now?'

'Good work, Biggs. The first thing is to get Angela out of this. Now, look here, my dear, are you game to make a bolt for it? It is your best chance, and if you can get clear, ring up the police and tell them that the Central Bank has been robbed and that the lorry bringing away the notes is due back here any minute. Don't say who you are; just make them realise it is urgent.'

'I am staying with you, sir,' broke in Biggs.

'Well, anyway, let's get down the stairs. Angela, when you get to the door, you run like hell, and we'll cover you behind.'

There was no time for discussion. Cautiously the three crept out of the door and down the stairs. On the first-floor landing they paused to brace themselves for the final descent to the street.

'What's that?' hissed Ferningham.

'Blimey, it's the old lady,' Biggs exclaimed, as, indeed, it was. For Mrs. Benson, who had just completed her sale, had sauntered with the now empty pram to the side entrance, and was even now looking up the stairs in despairing search of Biggs.

Like a flash of lightning an inspiration came to Ferningham.

'Nip down the stairs, Angela, and get in the pram! We are staying here!'

At the same time he signalled to Mrs.

Benson, whose mouth was already opening wide in astonishment. Angela did not waste a second, but hurried on down. A single stride from the next to bottom stair (the stairs rose, fortunately, direct from the door) and she was in the pram. Mrs. Benson, with surprising quickness of mind, threw the covering sacking over her. A signal from the two above bade her wait no longer, and with a magnificent nonchalance she wheeled her precious burden away.

Inwardly, during the first half-dozen yards, Mrs. Benson was bursting with excitement and with nervousness lest a voice from the yard should recall her. But there was no interruption, and without further mischance the landlady reached the corner. Here she paused for a moment and leaned against the wall. Exactly so, in years gone by, had she leaned against the wings after a triumphant exit from the stage . . . She wiped her forehead with a hand which trembled slightly, then, as she realised that the street was empty, she whipped the sacking from the pram.

'Quick, Miss Angela, there's no one about! Out you get!' Angela got out immediately and stretched herself luxuriously.

'Come on, my dear, we're only just round the corner!' The memory of Ferningham's last words came back to Angela as Mrs. Benson spoke, and immediately she was galvanised into activity.

'Now we've got to find a telephone.' They hurried along together for nearly half a mile, when suddenly Mrs. Benson stopped.

'There's a post office over there, Miss. Do you think that will do?'

'If the box is a private one, yes!' replied Angela cautiously. 'If you'll wait here I'll go in and see; and while I'm gone, please do get rid of that perambulator, Mrs. Benson. That is, unless you really have some use for it,' she could not help adding, as she realised that what to her was a small thing to throw away, might not be the same in the case of Mrs. Benson. But she need not have worried. With a rueful smile the landlady admitted that she, too, found its possession an embarrassing thing.

'Old as I am, Miss,' she confessed with a chuckle, 'it fair made me blush pushing this contraption along with Mr. Biggs. I'll come back for you here, Miss,' she finished, and without more ado she wheeled the compromising pram away. Where to dump it was the next question, as visions swept before her of people rushing after her with a warning that she had left her pram behind. At last she found the opportunity. A grocer's shop standing on a corner had a door facing on each street. She passed the first one, rounded the corner, and pulled the pram up beyond the second. Leaving it in the gutter she walked back and into the shop.

'Two candles, please,' she demanded, as being the cheapest purchase she could make.

'Penny, Ma,' said the youth behind the counter briefly. She found the penny with difficulty, having forgotten exactly where she had put her purse in her motley collection of skirts and sacking. Then, expecting to be recalled every moment, she escaped through the second door into the other street. Luckily, no one gave the alarm, and Mrs. Benson retraced her steps in triumph to the post office. Angela was already waiting for her on the pavement.

'I see you've managed to do it.' Mrs. Benson glanced down at her theatrical outfit. 'Pity I couldn't get rid of these clothes at the same time,' she replied, 'but there, I'm not exactly suited to be a Lady Godiva!'

Angela smiled. 'Well, I got through to Inspector Pateman and told him that a bank has just been robbed by the gang that were mixed up in the Kensington murder. I gave him the Waste Paper Factory address, and he's rushing police cars to surround it. He started to ask me some awkward questions, so I hung up.'

'In that case, Miss, we best be getting along home.'

'But we can't do that, Mrs. Benson! I can't leave here while Roger is in that factory. How is he going to find me when he gets out?'

Mrs. Benson laid a motherly hand on

the other's shoulder. 'I know, my dear, what you are feeling,' she answered quietly, 'but what good can your staying here do? When Major Ferningham gets out, as he will do, he'll come along home, you can be sure of that. It's a hard business, waiting is, but' — for once she spoke self-consciously — 'I can understand. I've got to wait for Biggs, Miss Angela.' She blew her nose violently as she finished, and Angela patted her arm in sympathy. Together they walked along in search of a taxi, both of them unusually silent as they wondered what was happening to their men.

But they need not have worried. Ferningham's greatest problem had been solved when he saw Angela escape, and as he stood upstairs on the landing he wiped his brow in relief.

'Thank heaven she's all right! Now, Biggs, if you're game we are going to have a slap at collecting that boodle. There should be a back way down to the wharf somewhere here.'

As he spoke he was trying a small door which lay at the back of the landing. It opened, disclosing a narrow flight of stairs. A musty smell of paper and river water came up the stairway. Ferningham led the way down. Half-way he paused.

'Did you bring a gun, Biggs?' he whispered. 'They took mine away from me.'

'Yes, sir. Here it is, sir. I would rather you have it, not being much of a hand with them myself.' As he spoke Biggs passed it over without any question, and they recommenced their descent. The next moment they were in the yard alone. On their left was a wharf with a narrow landing stage. Moored to this, and nearly filling the waterway, was a huge motor launch. The landing stage itself was piled high with suit cases. On their right lay the yard with its entrance to the cul-de-sac. Ferningham's heart missed a beat as he caught sight of a man not six yards away; the latter, luckily, had his back to them, keeping a watch out for the lorry's return. Ferningham silently gestured to the other, and together they crept along the landing stage towards the mouth of the wharf. As they reached the end of the pile of suit cases, Ferningham paused.

'Let's get behind these, and then we can keep a look-out,' he whispered in a low voice. 'I shouldn't think they'll be coming along here.'

'What have you got in mind, sir?'

'Well, this is what I am trying for. If Angela rings up the police all right, they should be here soon after the lorry. If the gang try to hold them up, we'll slip off in the launch with the boodle. If the gang try to clear off immediately, we've got to stop them at this end. In which case we should be heroes all right, but we shan't collect the cash. So let's hope they put up a fight in front.'

Biggs quivered with excitement. Forty minutes ago he had been in the throes of panic, and small blame to him. But now, as he would have termed it, he was out for blood. He was about to make some remark to this effect, when Ferningham interrupted him with a warning hiss. The look-out at the other end had suddenly sprung into activity. At the same moment could be heard the sound of a lorry approaching. The two stiffened in expectation. There was a sound of brakes and changing gear, then a sudden roar as the lorry entered the close confines of the yard. A comparative silence ensued as the driver switched off his engine. He could be heard descending from his cabin, and then a hurried conversation began as follows:

'Everything all right, Jake?'

'Sure, sweet as a nut — the whole thing was a cinch. Here, Bill, you start loading up the suit cases while I go tell the boss. There's a layer of waste paper on the top of each sack, and the rest are notes.'

Ferningham appeared round the covering barrier. At which end would they start? His fears were relieved the next moment as the driver's assistant and the watchman began at the other end of the pile. They wasted no time in words, but swinging a couple of sacks down they began feverishly to pack the first two suit cases. Ferningham turned to Biggs.

'If they can have five minutes of that, and then the police come along, we shall be all right. I don't think somehow that they will try to escape without the cash, which means that they will be busy holding up the police while one man is packing. We'll settle the man at the right moment, and take the launch. I can handle it all right.'

The above conversation was carried out in a series of pauses, to keep a watchful eye on the men working at the other end.

'But what's it all about, sir?' murmured Biggs in the lowest of whispers.

'The gang have robbed the Central Bank,' Ferningham explained. 'Those sacks of paper are sacks of notes. They are packing them in the suit cases and taking them down river somewhere, to a garage they've got. Then they're taking it out of London in forty or fifty cars; two suit cases to each car. That's why there are only about four of the gang here; the rest are at the garage.'

A sudden clamour from above cut him short. The next moment Jake came rushing down the stairs.

'Seen a fellow an' a girl?' he demanded breathlessly. The two packers straightened themselves incredulously.

'Man and girl? Hell, no! What's . . . '

'Then shut them goddamned doors!

Quick, and bolt them! If they've got adrift we'll have the police here in two shakes!'

Without waiting for the completion of his orders, he rushed back up the stairs and into the office. 'No sign, boss; I've told them to lock up below! Shall we go on looking about?'

'No,' replied the leader slowly; 'too late now! Get the machine gun out, and at the window. If the police come, we shall be ready for them.'

Jake hastened to obey. From a cupboard built into the wall, he pulled out a long oblong case and threw back the lid. Within twenty seconds he had a machine gun mounted on its tripod. Again he delved into the cupboard, and pulled out three or four small but heavy boxes full of ammunition. Deftly he filled up the machine-gun belt with cartridges and slipped it into position. Then, without bothering to open the window, he knocked out one of the small panes in the bottom sash so the machine-gun nozzle was able to protrude through the hole. Meanwhile, at the desk the leader was loading half a dozen revolvers from a box of cartridges.

'Here they come!' Jake burst into profanity. 'Shall I let 'em have it, boss?' But the leader was already by his side, and stooping to the gun, so that even as the police car straightened up after rounding the corner, the staccato brrup, brrup, brrup, of the machine gun burst forth! The police car lurched for a moment as it met that deadly hail, then, as the driver slipped sideways in his seat, the car, out of control, mounted the pavement, and, crashing into the wall, overturned.

'Some shootin', boss!' exclaimed Jake with ferocious glee.

'What's happening?' They both turned at the question to find a woman standing at the inner door of the office. It was the same Miss Wilkinson who until now had been in the employ of the Central Bank. Even now, beyond the natural surprise in her voice, she showed no signs of excitement.

'Police, my dear.' The leader spoke laconically, and knelt again by the gun. A renewed burst of fire emphasised his remark. 'Two of them were just getting out of the wreckage,' he explained. Without answering, the woman picked up a revolver from the desk, and crossed over to the window to the leader's side.

'Jake,' the latter ordered, 'go downstairs and tell Smith to carry on with the packing by himself. Tell him to hurry, and make sure that the doors are secure. Bring Davies back with you; we may need him up here.'

'Do you think the police know about the river entrance?' asked the woman as the door closed behind Jake.

'I don't know,' replied the other slowly, 'but it's as well not to discuss such a possibility in front of the men. They might want to leave now, and that does not suit me for a few minutes, at all events.' He broke off abruptly, and motioned the woman to the floor, in the same movement kneeling behind the gun. A second car had rounded the corner, but had pulled up short upon seeing the wreckage and the lifeless bodies beside it. Even as the machine gun came into action the occupants of the second car were clambering out and sheltering themselves behind it. There was a lull for a minute, then suddenly two figures broke from their hiding-place in an attempt to get back to the corner. The machine gun burst out again. The first man collapsed on his knees, seemed about to make a futile attempt to crawl the remaining distance, and then suddenly straightened himself in a last agony of life and collapsed. The other man stumbled too, as though he too was hit, but with the last effort he reached safety. Simultaneously, puffs of smoke from the rear of the car showed that the remaining police had come into action. There was a crash of glass and a whine as two bullets came through the window. The man and the woman crouched down behind the shelter of the window-sill. Downstairs, Jake was giving his orders. 'Drive that lorry back against the door, Bill. I don't suppose there'll be a rush, but you may as well be ready. Now, don't argue . . . everything's O.K. so long as you can get packed in five minutes! . . . Sure it's the police! But what of it? They can't get near us, at least not unless they want a chunk of lead in their bellies.' Bill sprang into the driver's cabin and started the engine. With a guiding hand from Jake he backed the lorry up against the door and sprang down again.

'That's swell, Bill. Now, you just carry on packing, and leave the rest to us. You come on up, Davies. We want as many guns as we can get upstairs.'

Down by the river entrance, Ferningham and Biggs had listened to the barrage with intense excitement.

'Shall we rush 'im now, sir?' whispered Biggs.

'Not yet,' came the reply. 'They've only got about a third packed. Let him carry on for two or three minutes. When he comes down here we'll get him. They'll be pretty busy upstairs, I should think.'

His assumption was correct. The policeman who had got to safety had warned the following patrols. A cordon had been thrown around the neighbouring streets to keep back the public, and a general call had been wirelessed for reinforcements. Now, from a near-by yard, a lorry had been procured and was being driven to the entrance of the cul-de-sac. As it came into view there was a renewed burst of fire from the factory windows, but the driver had crouched down under cover and the bullets rattled harmlessly through his windscreen. The lorry stopped, and thus formed a barricade behind which four policemen took up their position and began to open fire. Hardly had they done so before Pateman, who had not gone to bed that night at all, arrived on the scene. He took over from the inspector temporarily in charge and reviewed the situation. By this time he had twenty or thirty policemen with him, and with a thrill of exultation he thanked God that his chance had come. For he was certain that this robbery was one carried out by the same gang who had been responsible for the others. The important thing, however, was to capture one or more of the men alive. He made his way to the corner where a sergeant was unloading two boxes of ammunition from a police car.

'How many men are up there?' he demanded anxiously. 'Seem to be about four of them shooting, sir, but there is a machine gun at one of the windows.'

'How many casualties have we had so far?'

'Six, sir, up to the moment. Five of them are dead, too.' Pateman was aghast. At all costs he must endeavour to capture the factory without any further loss of life. With an order, therefore, for the sharpshooters behind the lorry only to maintain their fire so long as it was safe to do so, he went across the road and into a near-by house, which was built one storey higher than those around it.

'Is there any way on to the roof?' he asked the woman who came to the door.

'No, sir, but from the attic window you should be able to see out across to the factory,' she replied, realising the purpose of his question. She led the way up, and in a minute Pateman was at the window surveying the cul-de-sac. At once he realised that if the police could be sent over the roofs of the houses leading into the cul-de-sac, they would stand a good chance of working their way along under cover until they reached the factory itself.

Their one hope then was to get on to the roof of the factory, and if they were unable to get in from the roof itself, to work their way down and to climb in through the windows. While the machine gun continued in action it was impossible to rush the factory without the certainty of very heavy casualties.

He rejoined the others in the street. The crowd by now had reached mammoth proportions, and the cordon was having great difficulty in keeping them back. Pateman despatched a messenger who stood waiting for orders, to call up some much-needed reinforcements for the cordon itself. He then went along to the barricade.

The sergeant in command was worried. Already two of the sharpshooters had received minor flesh wounds, and at any moment more serious casualties might result. Pateman thought for a minute, and then went back to the builders' yard. Here, to his relief, were several sacks of sand lying about. Under his instructions they were rapidly carried to the corner and propped against the wheels of the lorry, thus forming an effective barrier against stray bullets, which had been coming under the chassis. A final inspection, and Pateman declared himself satisfied. He went back to the body of armed police which stood waiting for orders. After explaining what he wanted done by way of rushing the factory along the roofs of the houses, he called for volunteers. With the exception of one man they all stepped forward. The man in question weighed over fourteen stone, and, therefore, could not reasonably be expected to cope with roof climbing. Four of them were selected and started on their errand.

Upstairs in the attic Davies had taken over the machine gun, which he operated from the floor. At the other window knelt Jake, keeping up a continuous fire from the two guns which he carried. In the middle, standing up, but sheltered by the wall between the windows, the leader had taken his position, and was shooting from behind the curtain. In the centre of the floor crouched the woman beside the boxes of ammunition, and, as she loaded the spare guns she crawled over to the men to exchange them for their empty ones. Bullets were now coming through the windows in a continuous stream.

'Say, boss, they're getting along through the side houses . . . got you, you bastard!' Jake was right; the police had advanced in the shelter of the houses and there was a sudden outburst of firing from the near-by windows at almost the same level as those of the factory.

'See that, boss, they've got to our level now. Let's go!'

'Wait a minute, Jake, you were in always . . . ', but even as he spoke, Jake, who was in the act of crossing the room to gain the door, gave a sudden grunt and sank to the floor with a bullet through his back. ' . . . too much of a hurry,' finished the leader, with ironic calm. Jake made an effort to speak, but even as he opened his mouth there came a rush of blood. He coughed violently in a last paroxysm of effort. His head fell back, he grinned feebly as though at the grim jest, and the next moment was dead.

The room was full of smoke and dust

by now. Huge chunks of plaster had fallen from the ceiling and the walls as the bullets ploughed their deadly errand.

'Let's go, boss,' urged Davies, as he turned from the machine gun. 'Keep that gun going, and spray those windows.' It was a command rather than a reply. Then:

'Just keep them out for three minutes and we'll be away.'

Downstairs, Bill was already nine-tenths of his way through his packing. As each suit case was filled, he stowed it rapidly away in the well of the launch, pausing only to light a fresh cigarette. He had reached the last pile, and the moment had come. As his hand reached forward to take the top suit case, Ferningham stood up.

'What the . . . ' The man's sentence was never completed, for he fell back with a bullet through his head.

'Come along, Biggs,' Ferningham exclaimed, the smoking revolver still in his hand, and led the way to the launch. He stopped suddenly, seized with an idea, as he noticed for the first time a stack of petrol tins. He seized the nearest. It was full. Rapidly he unscrewed the top and poured the petrol over the stacks of paper in the yard. 'Get in the launch, Biggs,' he ordered. 'Do you know how to start her up? . . . You do? . . . Good; then get her going. A couple of minutes' blaze here, and those petrol tins will blow this dump to smithereens.'

Deliberately he waited for Biggs to start the motor, then casually threw a lighted match on the petrol-soaked piles. As the flames leaped up he hurried to the launch and jumped in behind the wheel.

'Well, Biggs, we're off to sea.'

'And not too soon, sir,' replied Biggs joyfully, as the boat swung out of the entrance and turned left towards the river mouth.

Biggs was right. Hardly had they cleared the entrance, when Davies, who had been sent down by the leader, arrived at the foot of the stairs. He gave an incredulous gasp at the sight which greeted his eyes. The flames were already roaring over half the yard and landing stage. Through the welter of smoke which belched from the stacks of paper he could barely see the water, but what he could see was enough! The landing stage was empty. The launch was gone!

Babbling incoherently, he tore back up the stairs and into the besieged office.

'The place is lit to Hades, boss, and the boat's gone!'

'You mean we're on fire?'

'Sure, blazing to hell, and the boat's gone — gone, I tell you!' His voice rose in terror. 'What'll we do, we can't die here like rats? Gimme a gun, boss, I'll show those b —s, gimme a . . . ', but even as he scrabbled on the floor in a frenzy of excitement for a gun, his words were cut short. That moment of excitement had left him a target for the bullets which rained into the room, and he collapsed with not one, but several, bullets in his body.

The leader turned to the woman who crouched on the floor beside him. With a surprising affectionate gesture he patted her arm, and shrugged his shoulders in mute acceptance of the facts. For a moment her face lit up, but not with fear. She, too, uttered no word, but merely passed him two more loaded guns. The police were now in the adjoining house. The machine gun had jammed a minute before. Now as they fired through the window, the police began to make their last effort. They had gained the roof above, and two were already climbing down a corner pipe to get in at the windows. An exclamation from the woman, and the leader turned to see a man in the act of straddling the window-sill, for the frames and glass had been long shot away. With a grunt, the leader shot from his hip. The man swayed for a moment, then fell head-long into the street below. Motioning the woman, the gangster backed to the rear of the room, and took cover behind the desk, whence he would have a better command of the windows.

'Not much longer now,' he murmured to his companion, still without a trace of excitement. They were his last words. There was a sudden roar, deafening in the extreme, as the flames reached the store of petrol below. The walls rocked for a moment, then as the intensity of the explosion was felt, the floor heaved, the room seemed grotesquely to lift itself, then with a final gigantic shudder everything collapsed!

★ ★ ★

A mile down the stream Ferningham checked the progress of the launch as he heard, even at that distance, the noise of the explosion. 'So perish all enemies,' he murmured, and with a light heart he set the nose of the launch for the open sea.

THE END